the resolution of
Callie & Kayden

JESSICA SORENSEN

For information:

jessicasorensen.com

Cover Design and Photography: Mae I Design

http://www.maeidesign.com/

The Resolution of Callie & Kayden (The Coincidence,
#6)

ISBN: 978-1495468414

Prologue

#103 Outrun Your Demons.

Kayden

Run.

Throw.

Catch.

Run.

Run.

Run.

My father's words scream from behind me as I sprint around the track. I can't outrun it, escape it, hide from the ghost memory of his voice. My feet pound against the ground as my lungs tighten in my chest, my entire body dripping with sweat even though it's barely fifty degrees outside and I'm wearing shorts. My pulse is pounding and my limbs ache, begging me to stop—that it's enough.

But nothing ever feels like it'll be enough.

Because I can't outrun the memory of his voice.

The words he drilled into me.

I want to be free from it—from him. Free from mom. My past. The years of abuse. What I really want is my resolution. But to get it, I'd need to let go of everything and I can't let go when my future is so unknown.

I don't know where my father is—what he's doing. If he's alive or dead. If he's sorry for what he did. And I might never know any of this. Just like I might never be able to let go of the past.

So all I can do is *run.*

Until I can no longer breathe.

Until my limbs can no longer move.

Until my heart stops beating.

And hope that one day maybe his voice will disappear.

Chapter 1
#101 Jump on the Bed. A Lot.

Callie

Wintertime is beautiful. Snowflakes tumble from the sky and swirl around in the air. They remind me that the world is always changing, that people are always changing, that I'm always changing. This reminder is what keeps me happy, keeps me moving forward in my life, allows me to let go of what happened with Caleb and live my life for the future. A future that is filled with endless possibilities.

Despite my positivity, I feel like something has been missing from my life lately, but I can't figure out what exactly it is. It's not necessarily a bad thing. In fact, it might be something good. Like sadness and perhaps pain. Or possibly that I'm moving more freely through life than I ever have. Or perhaps I'm just looking for something to explain this unfamiliarly new and liberating feeling residing in my heart, because the past seems so distant. The person who hurt me has vanished and even though there was no resolution for what Caleb did to me, I feel like my inner demons that are connected to him, and what he did, have been resolved. Yes, the memories are still there, scarring my past, but they don't define me anymore.

And I feel... well, happy.

I want to share this with Kayden, because he seems a little sad lately. Not like how he was before, though. No, he's much better than he was a year ago when I saw him in the clinic that horrible day. He was sent there because nurses and doctors thought he'd stabbed himself. While he had prior self-inflicted injuries, his father had been the one who'd inflicted the worst of them and had nearly killed Kayden and almost ruined the future he has now.

The beautiful one that we have now.

"Knock, knock, knock." Seth raps on my dorm room door as he cracks it open and sticks his head in. "Hey, what's up with you not answering your texts?"

I set the pen down in the spine of my journal and pick up my phone from the bed. "Sorry, I forgot I turned it down for class." I press the volume up while he fakes a pout and enters my dorm room.

He looks all kinds of Seth; stylish in his black and grey sweater, dark blue jeans, Converse sneakers, and his honey-blonde hair is tousled to perfection.

"Hot date tonight?" I set my phone down on the nightstand and shut my journal.

"Whatever do you mean?" He taps his finger on his lips, feigning ignorance, like he hasn't been chattering about his date with Greyson all week, the date that marks their year anniversary when they officially started considering themselves dating.

I tuck my journal underneath my pillow and hop off the bed and to my feet, smoothing out the creases in my violet and black striped shirt. "I mean, the date you've been yammering about for weeks now. *The* date. The one that marks your first anniversary."

He kicks the door closed. "You need to stop paying so much attention to me. It ruins all my fun and mysteriousness."

I reach for an elastic on my nightstand. "You're never mysterious," I say, putting my long, brown hair up in a ponytail. "But we can do a redo if you want to. You can go back out of my room and enter again, and I can pretend that I have no idea why you're dressed up. Then you can announce the news to me, and we can celebrate and jump up and down and scream, 'Oh my God!' " I wave my hands in front of me while I bounce up and down. "It's going to be so epically awesome!"

He stares at me for a moment, pretending to be irritated, but then the corner of his mouth turns upward, and he starts jumping up and down with me. "Let's just skip to the good part." He laughs as he leaps up onto my bed and bounces on the mattress, offering his hand to help me up.

"Why, thank you, sir." I grab his hand, and he pulls me up with him.

We continue to jump on the bed like kids, yelling about his anniversary until my roommate, Harper, strolls into the room. She stops dead in her tracks at the sight of us, jumping on the bed, red-faced and panting with our hands in the air.

"Hey, Harper." I wave at her as I cease jumping. Seth continues, though, unbothered that he looks like a complete lunatic, but he also doesn't have to share a room with Harper for the entire year either.

Harper's gaze flicks between Seth and me as she steps into the room and closes the door behind her. "What are you guys doing?" she asks, intrigued.

Seth begins to exaggeratedly bounce on the bed. "Exercising," he jokes breathlessly.

"Great idea. I'll have to try it sometime. Although, I'm a two person kind of jumping-on-the-bed girl myself. " Harper winks, but something about it looks wrong, like she's just playing a part instead of being herself—she's that way a lot.

She walks over to the desk near the window to set her books down while Seth giggles at her remark and I feel a blush rush to my cheeks. Even now, after I've had sex, I still get embarrassed over sexual innuendos. I used to think it was because I was raped when I was twelve by my brother's then best friend and it had left that kind of a mark on me, but I'm coming to realize that it might just be my personality.

"So what are you two up to for the day?" Harper asks as she pulls her long, blonde hair into a messy bun before picking up her iPod from her bed.

Seth shrugs as he hops off the bed and lands on the floor with a thud. "Not anything right now. Why? You looking for a party buddy again?"

She wavers, slightly distracted as she shuffles through the list of songs on her iPod. "I was thinking about going to this frat party tonight, but I'm still on the fence about it."

Seth makes a gagging face as he mock clutches his neck. "Frat boys. Yuck."

"For sure," she agrees, reaching for her headphones that are on her pillow. "But I need to get out of this tiny box-of-a-room for a night or I'm going to go crazy."

"Well, sorry, but you're going to have to ride solo on this one Hun," Seth tells her. The two of them occasionally see each other at parties and hang out, but that's as far as their friendship stems.

"Bummer." She smiles at me, but it doesn't reach her eyes. "What about you, Callie? You down for a party?"

"I'm with Seth on this one," I reply, feeling kind of guilty when she frowns. "I'm not into frat parties."

She shrugs it off, seeming a bit depressed. But once she catches me noticing her plummeting cheeriness, she forces a bright smile then pops her earbuds in. I'm not sure why, but Harper seems lonely all the time, even though she's always surrounded by people. She keeps smiling as she moves for her bed, but I've given enough fake smiles in my life to recognize one when I see it.

As she flops down and gets situated to do her homework, Seth waves at her then takes me by the elbow and steers me toward the door. "Let's go get some coffee," he says, grabbing my hoodie from the bedpost and shoving it at me, "and I'll tell you about the present I got Greyson."

Slipping on my jacket, I follow Seth out the door and down the slender hallway to the elevators and then step inside.

"So it's a collection of things we've done together," he says as I push the button to the bottom floor. "Like DVDs we've watched, music we've listened to, food we both

12

agree is awesome."

"That might be the coolest present ever."

"I know, right?"

I nod as we exit the elevator and enter the lounge area. Then we stroll toward the front door and exit outside. It's a breezy yet beautiful day to be walking beneath the crystal blue sky. Frost clings to the branches of the leafless trees that surround the dorm building, and the frozen grass makes the entire scene look like a winter wonderland.

"So what's new with you?" Seth asks as we veer in the direction of the nearest coffee shop, which is kitty-corner from the University of Wyoming—a college in Laramie that we both attend. "It feels like ages since I've talked to you."

I laugh because it's only been like a day. "Not much."

"How's the new job going?"

I sigh. I got an internship writing for an online news-paper at the beginning of the semester. I love writing and everything but… "It's kind of not what I was expecting," I tell him as we leave the grass and step onto the slippery sidewalk.

"What do you mean?" he asks and we link arms before one of us wipes out on the ice.

I give a half shrug. "I wish I could just write, I don't know, whatever I want instead of about certain things. It

13

feels like such a job." I sigh. "That makes me sound selfish, doesn't it? And ungrateful."

Seth chuckles as he maneuvers us around a large ice patch. "No, it makes you sound normal. You don't have to like a job just because you have a job."

I tuck my free hand into the pocket of my jacket as the wind bites at my skin. "Yeah, I guess you're right."

"No, you don't guess I'm right; I *am* right." He shoots me a conceited grin. "I'm always right when it comes to advice." A thoughtful look crosses his face. "Which, speaking of advice, why haven't you talked to Kayden about moving in together? I thought we talked about that a couple of weeks ago, and you were going to finally"—he makes an air quote with his free hand—"go for it."

I internally cringe at the painful reminder. "I already told you I decided not to."

"I know, but I was hoping you would change your mind. I think you're wrong about Kayden not being ready for that big of a step, and even if he isn't ready, I still think you should know where he stands." He pauses as we halt at the corner of the sidewalk, waiting to cross the street. "You guys have been together way longer than Greyson and I, or Luke and Violet."

"Yeah, but the four of you all live together—they don't

just live by themselves." I know I'm giving him an excuse, but I don't want to think about the truth right now because it kind of hurts.

"You want us to all get a place?" Seth questions as we shuffle off the curb and cross the street to the quaint looking coffeehouse that has one of the best mocha cappuccinos I've ever had.

I shake my head. "Six people under one roof is way too much."

"Good, because I really didn't want to," he says with a playful nudge in my side. "I just didn't want to seem like a jerk."

"You're not a jerk," I tell him as I jump up onto the curb. "You're the bestest friend ever."

"You're so right." He points a finger at me. "Just like I'm so right about needing to talk to Kayden and see where your future lies." He steers us around a car pulling out of the coffee shop. "I love that guy to death, but he needs to start expressing how he feels more instead of always leaving you guessing."

"Kayden's good to me," I say defensively. "He's just had a lot of stuff happen to him, and I think it makes it hard for him to trust people."

Annoyance fills Seth's expression. "You've been through a lot of stuff too, and that's something you both need to remember."

"Seth, please, just drop it, okay?" I hope he can't read me as well as he usually does because I don't want to talk about this anymore.

He studies me suspiciously. "You're keeping something from me," he says as we arrive at the coffee shop door, but instead of walking inside, he halts and makes me halt with him. "Okay, Miss Callie, fess up. What aren't you telling me?"

A stray strand of my hair falls into my face as I try to keep my gaze averted from him, but I've never been a good liar and within seconds, I end up breaking down beneath his withering stare.

"Okay fine." I blow out a breath as I look at Seth. "I do know for sure that Kayden doesn't want to live with me because I asked him at the beginning of the year."

"What!" he exclaims, dropping his hold on me. "Why am I only hearing about this now?"

I inch toward the railing as someone exits out the door. "Because I didn't really feel like talking about it."

He frowns as he puts his elbows on the railing and reclines against it. "Well, what exactly did Kayden say? Just straight up 'no, I don't want to live with you'?"

"Well, he didn't straight up say it like that. I just said

something about how it'd be cool to live in an apartment next semester and how I was thinking about it, but I needed a roommate… and he didn't say anything."

Seth relaxes as he shakes his head and restrains a grin. "My dear, darling, naïve Callie. Implying something isn't the same as asking." He pats my head like I'm a child. "And when it comes to guys, you have to make sure to be really straightforward with what you want. Trust me. I have to deal with it all the time with Greyson."

"Yeah, you're probably right." I move back as Seth reaches around me and opens the door. "It's just really hard putting myself out there like that because what if Kayden does give me a flat out no?"

I walk inside the coffeehouse and Seth follows me, letting the door swing closed and shutting out the cold. The air smells like fresh coffee and cinnamon, and the sounds of clicking keyboards flutter around us since many students come here to use their laptops for the free Wi-Fi.

"I don't think he will say no," Seth says as we get in line.

I stare at the menu above the countertop, trying to figure out what to order. "I'm not so sure…" I move forward with the line. "He's been really sad and kind of distant lately."

"Then ask him why. Callie, come on. I know this is

17

your first relationship, but you guys are close enough that there shouldn't be this much space between you." When I start to open my mouth to protest, he adds, "Hey, you have to listen to me. I'm now officially a psych major and know what I'm talking about."

I choke on a laugh. "I hate to break it to you, but just because you're majoring in psychology doesn't mean you know everything."

"I know that." He puts two fingers to his temple. "It's this bad boy right here that makes me so damn insightful."

I shake my head but smile. Regardless of Seth being a know-it-all right now, he is right—I do need to talk to Kayden. "All right, I'll do it," I say.

"You better. And besides, living in an apartment is way, *way* better than living in the dorms. And you can be super noisy whenever you want." He waggles his eyebrows at me.

Despite my blush, I decide to play along. "Oh, I know. That's the main reason I want to move in with Kayden—so I can have some alone time without worrying about room-mates walking in on us."

He gives me the biggest grin ever. "Look at my baby girl. All grown up."

I stand up straighter. "Now, if I could just get the balls

to ask Kayden then I'd finally be getting somewhere."

Seth's face turns red as he works to stifle his laughter, but it gets the best of him, and he hurries and conceals his mouth with his hand. "I cannot believe you just said balls."

"You know what?" I say as we reach the register. "I *can* believe it. I'm not the same girl I used to be."

As he lowers his hand from his mouth, his humor dissolving. "You're so right. You have changed. You're so much stronger now."

Even though it's our turn to order, we give each other a hug. "We've both come so far," I say because Seth's had his own struggles and yet here we are—happy, healthy, and enjoying life. Survivors, that's what we are. I just wish Kayden could see that about himself. Realize just how far he's come.

Maybe Seth's right. Maybe it's time to eliminate that little space between Kayden and me. After all, I have faced worse than asking my boyfriend to move in with me.

Way, way worse.

Chapter 2

#107 Have a Winter Wonderland Magical Moment.

Kayden

I've been in a downer of a mood lately. It's nowhere near the same as it used to be when I'd get so down I'd lock myself in the bathroom and cut the pain out by slicing my skin open and letting myself bleed. I won't go back to that place no matter what happens to me. I refuse to live in the dark hole ever again. I want things to remain light. I just wish I could fully grasp onto life like Callie grasps onto it, but there are some things—fears—holding me back. An abundance of things bother me when I really start to analyze them. Like the fact that Thanksgiving is in less than a month, making it almost a year since my father stabbed me then bailed with my mother before he could pay the consequences. It was the around the same time when my already crumbling life fell apart. When I just about gave up and ended it all.

But I didn't. I survived, and I should be grateful, which I am, but it still bothers me that my father and mother are who-knows-where, doing who-knows-what, maybe without a care in the world.

Then there's the fact that my oldest brother Dylan invited me to his house for Thanksgiving to a *family* dinner. I'm not sure what to do with that one, how to react to the word *family*. I can't even picture the concept of sitting around the table with my brother and his wife and all of her family, laughing and chatting while we stuff our stomachs with food. Dylan said he would have invited Tyler too, but neither of us has seen him in quite a while. We both are worried that he's addicted to drugs, living on the streets somewhere like he's done before. Or worse, maybe he's not alive at all.

I feel like I'm stuck in the past, and I want to move forward. My therapist tells me all the time that I need to. But it's more complicated than it seems and depressing to take in sometimes—the lack of family I have and the fact that I'll never truly have a group of people there for me.

There is one person who always gets me through my despair, though.

Callie Lawrence.

She's the best thing that's ever happened to me—my ray of sunshine through the rain, the clouds, the storm that's hovered over my head. She can make me smile when I'm down, laugh when I'm unhappy. She's the one person who has ever loved me and who I completely and wholly love back in a way I can barely understand sometimes because I honestly thought I could never love anyone like the way I love her. That I'd never know how to love since I never really learned how to. Yet Callie showed me how to open my heart—at least, when it comes to loving her. She makes it so easy, and sometimes, it confuses me because why couldn't my family just do it—love each other instead of being so full of ugly hatred?

"Kayden, get your head into practice!" my coach hollers as he motions at me to get my ass on the field. I've been standing on the sidelines, staring at the end zone for who knows how long, lost in my thoughts.

Getting my head back into practice mode, I jog to the center of the field, hooking the chin strap on my helmet as I join my other teammates in the huddle. We're in our practice uniforms, the field icy from last night's intense temperature drop, and it's fucking cold. But it's good to be outdoors, distracting myself from my thoughts that haunt me whenever I'm in my room alone. Playing clears my head more than anything else, except for maybe talking to Callie, who I get to see when practice is over.

Still, even when I'm playing, I can hear the faintness of *his* voice telling me what to do. It's always there whenever I'm doing anything athletic and sometimes when I'm asleep. I hate that I hear it, but after years of it being drilled in my mind, I can't get rid of the sound.

Run.

Do better.

Go faster.

Play harder.

Keep going until you break.

It's only when I'm dripping with sweat and exhausted that I can barely hear my father's voice in my head, my heart thudding too loudly to hear anything else. It makes me love/hate football—love it for me, but hate it because it's connected to my father.

Still, I focus on what I need to do for practice, putting my heart into playing well, running the drills, throwing, catching, playing as good as I always do. By the time we're finished and I'm heading to the locker room, the sweat has soaked through my uniform and my body is tired and my brain is also too exhausted to think so I'm feeling pretty good. Coach pulls me aside before I go in and tells me how good I'm doing, but then gives me some things to work on. He usually does this, but he's been on my case a lot more this year since we've been playing so well. There's been a lot of talk about my future in football, even though I'm still a sophomore and still have a ways to go before the draft

23

comes into my sights. I'm grateful for the time too because I'm not even sure that I want to do it anyway. My whole life my dad threw me into sports and I always excelled at them, so it just seemed like that was the path I'd follow. And I love playing. But sometimes I wonder if there's more to life than this. If maybe there's something out there for me that's not linked to my father's dream for me and the sound of his voice constantly haunting me with every run and throw I make.

After I go to the locker room, I take a quick shower and change into a pair of jeans and a T-shirt. Then I slip my jacket on and head out to the parking lot toward my car. It's not the best looking car in the world, but it's better than my motorcycle and gets me to places. Plus, the great part is I bought it myself with the money I make from the part time job I have at the local gym. It's all mine. My own little pride and joy. Not my father's.

When I climb inside, I turn on the engine and toss my bag into the backseat. It's getting late, the sun starting to descend behind the mountains, so I flip on the headlights before I push the car into drive. I'm about to pull out of the parking lot when my phone buzzes inside my pocket.

Pressing on the brake, I stop the car near the exit to take my phone out of my pocket, smiling because I know who the text is from before I even check it.

Callie: Hey! Where r u? I thought we were supposed to meet at your dorm at seven, but you're not here...

Me: Sorry, I'm running a little late. Coach wanted to talk about stuff.

I frown for the intentional avoidance of the subject. I haven't talked to Callie about the uncertainty of my future in football—or the uncertainty in my future period. She's always really positive and knows exactly what she wants out of life and it makes it difficult to talk to her about stuff.

Me: R u at my dorm right now?

Callie: Yeah, in your room... Niko let me in.

I pull a face at the mention of my roommate. Not that I don't like him or anything, but he has some serious issues and he's high half the damn time.

Kayden: Is he with u right now?

Callie: No, he just left... why?

Kayden: Just wondering... I'm heading there now. Be there in like 10.

Callie: K :) And I have something really important I want to talk to you about... It's about us.

I grow uneasy, wondering what she wants to tell me, afraid she might want to take a break from us or something else equally as bad. I really don't think that's it, but my mind always seems to go to that dark place whenever there's something unknown in front of me. I can't help worrying that Callie will hurt me because she has the power to do it. She owns my heart and soul completely, and she could easily break me.

Lost in my worries, I pull out onto the road and drive toward my dorm building. By the time I'm parking the car, it's snowing like a blizzard. Massive snowflakes splatter against the windshield and instantly soak through my clothes as I hop out and jog across the frosted grass to the entrance doors. Then I breathe in the warmth as I step into the foyer area.

Halloween is nearing and everything is decorated in black and orange, and there are fake spider webs everywhere along with this stupid skeleton that makes spooky noises every time someone walks by it. There are a few people sitting around in the lounge area, laughing and talking, a couple of which I know, so I give them a wave and say hello before going to the elevator.

The closer I get to my room, the more eager I am to touch Callie, wishing I could do it all the time. Unfortunately, I'm not in the same dorm building as her, and it makes staying together all night a pain in the ass. Honestly, it'd be easier if we just lived together, but that is one hell of a big step, and I'm not sure if I'm—we're—ready for that or if she'd even want to.

When I arrive at my room, I punch in the code and walk inside, smiling before I even see her. But I frown when I step over the threshold and discover that the room is vacant, just two unmade twin beds, some empty Dorito bags on the floor, and a lot of Coke cans on the dresser. The mess makes me miss Luke as a roommate and his need to keep everything clean and organized.

There's also a stack of DVDs on my nightstand, which I'm assuming Callie brought over since they weren't here earlier. *So where the hell is she?*

I'm scratching my head, wondering why she'd leave, when my phone vibrates from inside my pocket. My eyebrows knit together as I retrieve it and swipe my finger across the screen.

Callie: Put your coat on and meet me outside on the east side of the campus yard.

Me: Why does this sound so suspicious... you're not planning my murder r u?

Callie: Not tonight. I saved my roll of duct tape and shovel for another day ;)

I can't help chuckling at her adorableness.

Me: All right. Just as long as no shovel and tape are involved then I'll b out in a few :)

27

Callie: k, see ya soon :)

I stuff my phone back into my pocket, pondering what she could be up to. She's been so happy lately, even with the fact that Caleb—the guy who raped her when she was twelve—is still out there somewhere in the world, living his life, not paying for what he did to not just Callie, but Luke's sister as well, along with a few others. And there's a chance he won't ever have to pay for what he did to them. He'll just go on living his life, doing whatever he wants, while his victims are left to cope with his destruction. It's a huge flaw in life and one I understand way too well.

Shaking the depressing thought from my head, I tug my beanie over my brown hair before I depart out the door and toward the cold again. I try to stay upbeat as I take the elevator to the bottom floor, go back outside, and wind around the building, heading where Callie instructed. The leafless trees around the building are decorated with lights that reflect against the ice covering everything. It's freaking freezing out here, my breath puffing out in a cloud. I should have worn a heavier coat. I'm thinking about turning back and dressing more warmly when I step out into the open area on the east side and suddenly I stop caring that I'm outdoors and freezing my ass off.

Callie is standing in the middle of the frosted trees,

lights, and benches, staring down at the ground with the hood of her coat down and her hands in her pockets. Snowflakes speckle in her long brown hair and she's kicking at the snow with the tip of her boot, seeming lost in her thoughts.

She's so beautiful.

Amazing.

Perfect.

I give myself a moment to appreciate everything that's her before I hike toward her and make my presence known. She must hear my boots crunch against the snow because her gaze lifts and finds me before I reach her. Snow dots her eyelashes, her cheeks are flushed, and she has a smile on her face, her eyes so full of love that I seriously about turn around and look over my shoulder to make sure there's no one else standing there that she might be looking at.

"Hey, you," she says, still grinning at me. Then she shifts her weight and a hint of her nerves slips through, which instantly makes me nervous.

Why would she be nervous?

"Hey you back." My feet move toward her on their own, wanting—*needing*—to be near her. "Why are you standing out here in the freezing cold?"

She holds up her finger, indicating to wait a second. Then she glances at the leafless, snow-bitten tree beside her before she ducks behind it. A heartbeat later, music envelops me. When she steps back out from behind the tree, she's smiling as the snowflakes swirl around us, almost moving with the slow rhythm of the song.

"What do you have back there?" I ask. "An iPod dock or something?"

She shakes her head as she walks through the snow toward me, reducing the space between us, something I'm ridiculously grateful for. In fact, I want it all gone—not a single drop of space left between our bodies.

"No, it's Luke's stereo. Seth borrowed it from him so I could use it for this."

My smile rises, the first one I've had all day. "God, he's so weird with all that old crap he keeps around, right?"

"Like all his mixed tapes?" she says with a soft laugh as she stops in front of me and tips her head back to look up at me.

I put my hands on her hips and eliminate the rest of the space between us. Suddenly, I become warm in the midst of the cold. "I seriously think he belongs in the 80s."

"Maybe he does." She loops her arms around the back of my neck and draws me nearer. "What era do you think we'd belong in if we could go live in a different one?"

I consider what she said. "How about the 60s?"

She beams up at me. "We'd be all about the peace, love, and happiness."

"I think that sounds a lot like you." I tuck a strand of her damp hair behind her ear. "I'm not sure about me, though."

Her forehead creases as I stroke her cheek with my finger, mesmerized by the softness of her skin. I've touched it a thousand times and every time is as amazing as the first.

"You've seemed a little bit down lately," she says. "Has something been bothering you?"

"I've just been thinking about some stuff." I trace a path up her jawline to her temple where she has the smallest birthmark.

"About family stuff?" she asks, shivering from my touch.

"Yeah... I can't help it... with the holidays coming. It's just got me thinking."

"About your family?"

I swallow the stupid lump that wedges its way up my throat. "Yeah, about my lack of one." I don't really mean to say it because I don't want to be a downer when clearly she had some sort of fun night planned, but it just slips out.

"You have me," she says quietly, placing a hand on my stubbly cheek. "You always will."

My heart tightens in my chest. "I know I do." I just wish it were that simple, that I did fully believe she'd always be here with me, that nothing would change and that could be enough in life. But I've been abandoned before, so there's a bit of a skeptic in me.

Still, being here with her momentarily lifts my problems away, and I lean in to kiss her, unable to take the space between us any longer. However, she quickly pulls away, stopping mid-kiss, and leaving me panting for air.

"What's wrong?" I ask.

She lets out a shaky breath, jittery and shivering from the cold. "I have to ask you something… something really, really important."

I search her eyes, and I see the same nerves I noticed when I first walked up to her. "What's wrong?"

She takes another unsteady breath and her hold on me intensifies, her fingers digging into the fabric of my coat, like she's afraid to let me go. "Okay, so I have something I want you to think about, but I don't want you to answer it tonight."

"Okay…?" I'm trying not to get worried, but it's hard when she's acting this way.

Her eyes are wide and full of terror, yet she refuses to break her gaze. "Okay, so I've been thinking a lot about our... our living situation." Her chest rapidly rises and falls, causing fog to rise around her face. "Remember how at the beginning of the school year I mentioned something about how much easier it'd be if we were living together?"

I waver because I don't really remember what she's talking about, but it seems like maybe I should. "I vaguely remember you saying something about you wanting to move out of the dorm and get your own apartment."

A loud exhale puffs from her lips. "Well, what I meant to say when I said it... or what I should have just flat-out said is maybe we should just... you and I"—she gestures between the two of us—"live... together..." she trails off, biting her lip, which has turned a bit blue from the cold.

I swallow hard, unsure how to answer. I have no idea how I feel about the idea. Excitement. Want. God, the want. But I'm fucking conflicted because within the want there's also fear.

Am I ready for that?

Yes.

No.

Yes.

No.

Maybe.

Shit.

Why can't I just give her what she wants?

She deserves that.

Deserves more.

I'm feeling way too much at the moment. The old Kayden would be bailing out by now and running back to his room to find a razor because it'd be the easiest way to deal with this—or not deal with it, anyway. But I don't want to become that guy again.

Callie watches me with hope while I struggle to sort through the confusion flowing through my mind. My lips part to try to explain to her what's going on, even though I'm guessing it's going to be a jumble of nonsense, but she quickly covers my mouth with her hand.

"Don't answer me right now." She slowly lowers her hand from my lips. "Just think about it. Talk to your therapist and figure out if you really want to do it or not," she says with a shrug. "I was just letting you know that I want to."

I nod, freeing a trapped breath. "Okay, I'll think about it."

Her lips curve into a smile then she stands on her tiptoes to place a kiss on my mouth. Her taste drowns me, and for the slightest, liberating moment, I forget about everything. The kiss is too quick, though, and when she starts to pull away, I cup the back of her neck and pull her right back to me, refusing to let her go, wanting to feel the calmness inside me just a little bit longer.

She doesn't protest as I slide my tongue deep inside her mouth, exploring every inch while grasping onto her hips, gripping her sides. She clutches onto me tightly in response, our bodies aligning as snow falls around us, soaks through the fabric of clothes to our skin while soft music continues to play in the background.

It's one of those easy moments with her that I look forward to, and I wish I could stay in it forever. Yet, for some reason, I have a feeling the snow is going to stop falling and life will move on.

Move forward.

To a future.

I just wish I knew what the hell I'm supposed to do.

Chapter 3

#117 Don't Let the Cursor Torture You.

Callie

It's getting close to Halloween, and I want to dress up for it. I haven't actually dressed up since I was eleven, the last time I felt like a child. I know I'm not a child now, but having my childhood stolen from me, I want to have some fun. And Seth wants me to go to a Halloween concert thingy with Greyson, him, Luke, and Violet. A couple's Halloween/dance/costume concert. I agree, but tell him I'll have to talk to Kayden, unsure if it's his kind of thing.

I probably like the idea too much and shouldn't be getting my hopes up until I know for sure if he'll go, but I never got to do the whole prom thing, never got to wear something that made me look pretty, didn't really believe I was pretty nor did I want to be at the time, never wanted to draw that kind of attention to myself. I never got to dance with a guy I loved and who looked at me like I was the most beautiful thing in the world. And I want all of that for just one night.

Seth coaxes me into going shopping for a costume before I get the chance to ask Kayden, but I don't mind. In fact, I'm having fun looking for something to wear. Although, Seth seems to think he needs to put in his two cents, and let's just say that his costume ideas are... well, a little bit too daring and bold for my taste.

"Yeah, I'm not sure Kayden would go for the whole Peter Pan/Tinkerbell thing," I tell Seth when he holds up a costume that includes green tights and curly toed shoes.

He gives me an innocent smile, shoving the costume at me. "Why ever not?"

I roll my eyes as I continue to search the rack in front of me. "Um, because it includes tights. That's why." I move hangers to the side as I look through the choices. "Besides, I don't want to be Tinkerbell."

Seth frowns disappointedly. "Yeah, but Kayden wears those super tight pants when he plays football, which is pretty much the same as tights."

I laugh as I sift through the slutty looking options of costumes, none of which I'm ready for, nor do I think I'll ever be ready for. "Yeah, and I've caught you checking him out before in those super tight pants, buddy. You are so not as discreet as you think."

"Who says I was trying to be discreet?" he retorts, putting his hands on his hips. "I was just admiring the view.

37

And don't pretend like you don't do it, too—admire a nice ass when you see one."

As my cheeks warm, he laughs at me, amused by my embarrassment. Still chuckling, he wanders around the racks filling the small store, searching for a costume. The selection is pretty picked over, and there a lot of people skimming through the already limited supply.

"So have you decided on one yet?" Seth asks a minute or two later, backing away from a rack and rubbing his stomach. "Because I'm getting super hungry."

I shake my head as I pull a face at a thin piece of leather that's supposed to be some sort of dress yet looks more like a really short shirt. "The problem is, I don't want to be something scary or slutty, and that's all they really have here."

He glances over at the wall of masks then at the rack I was just looking through. "That sort of eliminates a lot of options, if not all of them."

"I know," I sigh, glancing around the store. "I just want to be something pretty. Something that's not slutty, but is sort of sexy in a way where I don't have to show a lot of skin, if that makes sense. Something that will... dazzle Kayden." I grin at my word usage because dazzle is one of Seth's favorite words.

He bobs his head up and down to the music playing in the store, then looks around contemplatively. "That actually makes perfect sense for you." He takes my hand. "Come with me, beautiful. I think I have an idea for the perfect costume for you. One that will make you" —he grins at me— "dazzle the whole entire world."

I smile as I follow him out of the store, hoping that today's efforts will be worth it, that somehow I can make the night magical, or at least get Kayden to smile. That alone would make all my efforts worth it.

Later that day, I return to my dorm room with a bag that's holding what I think will be the perfect costume. I know I'm being silly, that I'm almost twenty and should not be getting excited over a silly party, but I am.

Last Halloween, Kayden and I technically weren't boyfriend and girlfriend. Yeah, we were hanging out, but that was about it. And then about a month later, around Thanksgiving, everything fell apart. It started when Kayden found out what Caleb had done to me when I was twelve. He'd gotten so angry that he beat up Caleb and ended up getting arrested for it. Then Kayden's father had stabbed him for getting in trouble with the police. It was a terrible, horrible time I know Kayden still thinks about a lot, even though he doesn't talk to me about it too much. Because of his crappy past, I want the end of this year and future ones to be fun for him—for the both of us. Plain and simple fun.

After I put my bags away, I turn on my iPod, hitting random before popping my headphones on. "Winter Song" by Sara Bareilles and Ingrid Michaelson clicks on, totally fitting for the storm outside. Then I get my laptop from the nightstand and plop down onto the bed.

I do a little writing for my internship, but after getting bored with it, I change documents and work on a story for my portfolio. The theme is fiction, but Professor Gladsyman pressed that we should write about something that feels real, something that's resting on the line between fiction and nonfiction.

Sometimes, I feel...

Yeah, that's all I have so far. It's not like I'm having writers block. Okay, well maybe I am, but it's not only that. Writing the vague truth, that's the hard part. But I'm not even supposed to be writing the truth, am I? Honestly, I'm kind of confused which route I'm supposed to go, especially since the professor kept making air quotes whenever he said fiction. I swear he wanted the class to be able read his mind and figure it out on our own.

Sighing, I delete my whole three words and then take

up the hobby of staring at the blank screen and that damn blinking cursor, the one that I swear is whispering, *you better find an idea,* over and over again, though not to encourage me—to torture me. Every time I try to get it to stop, the voice only grows louder, and I swear to God, I'm going crazy—writer crazy.

After a while, I get up and get a snack from my dresser drawer then take out my dress—aka my costume—and admire it again, totally procrastinating.

When I tried the dress on in the store, I felt like a gothic princess. Yeah, it was a cliché thought—well, minus the gothic part—but I welcomed it, remembering how I used to dream of being a princess and going to prom before it got squashed. After I was raped, I shut down completely, living only within myself. I chopped off my hair and only spoke to my journal for the most part, everything I was feeling pouring out through a pen. That's what I did until I left for college, which means that all that high school stuff I convinced myself was silly never happened and now I regret missing out on it.

"It could be like prom for you," Seth had said when he was attempting to convince me that this dress was, indeed, what I needed to wear. "And you could be like Cinderella and lose your glass slipper so Kayden has to find you and give it back."

I'd been holding the dress up to myself and gazing at my reflection in a store's mirror. "Seth, this is just a party. And this is definitely not a dress Cinderella would wear."

"Then be Callierella," he said with a wink. "Or Calliepunzel and you can lock yourself in your bedroom until Kayden begs that you let him inside."

I snorted a laugh. "Are you drunk? I mean, I know you had a Margarita at lunch, but it usually takes a lot more to get you tipsy."

"I'm not drunk," he said, snatching the dress from my hand. "I'm just trying to give you the fairytale you deserve."

"Life isn't a fairytale," I replied, but in the end, I bought the dress, kind of wishing life was.

If life were a fairytale, I think to myself as I hang up the dress in the closet, *it would be a lot darker and more twisted. I mean, some of those fairytales have a dark side; an evil villain, a wicked dilemma to get over, like a curse. But I'd never want to be a princess, at least not the kind that waits around for a prince to save her.*

I'd want to save myself. And maybe the prince as well. Maybe we could save each other.

An idea sparkles inside my mind, and I let out an excited clap and cheer. "Holy crap, I've got it!"

Right then, Harper enters the room with a bag slung over her shoulder. She gives me a weird look as she sets her card key down on the dresser and her bag on the bed. *You okay?* She mouths because I have my headphones in.

I nod eagerly as I skip back to my bed. "Yeah, just got a really cool idea." Then I turn to the computer and place my fingers on the keyboard, listening to the voice inside my head that belongs not to a cursor, but a character as I type the first three words.

The Truthful Fairytale.

Chapter 4

#101 Don't Let Your Family Get to You.

Kayden

Working at the gym isn't what I want to do for the rest of my life, but it gives me a cash flow so it works for now. It's always loud and has this weird smell I never notice when I'm working out, but can barely breathe through it when I'm working. It usually takes me at least an hour before my nostrils get used to it. Today, though, it's giving me a headache, or maybe that's just because I didn't sleep very well last night. I want to lie down on the floor and go to sleep, but instead, I have to stand at the front counter for four hours straight and talk to people when they need help.

My phone's been buzzing in my pocket all day, but I can't answer it until I take my break. I think it might be Callie, and it's driving me insane because I want to talk to her, yet I don't. After our conversation the other day about moving in together, I've been worried about what she'll say, afraid she's going to ask me what my decision is, and I'm going to have to tell her that I have no clue. My only hope left is to maybe sort out my jumbled thoughts at my therapy appointment tomorrow.

Finally, at a little after two o'clock, I get my break. After putting on my jacket, I step out the back door and into the cold. The sky is grey and the snow is refusing to stop or melt, piling up on the roads. I wonder just how intense the winter's going to be. Usually, it doesn't even start snowing until November, but it's the end October and there's already a shitload.

My phone vibrates again as I'm cutting across the icy parking lot toward my car. I rummage around in my pocket for it then start dial Callie's number when I see the screen and realize all the missed texts and calls aren't from her, but from my older brother Dylan.

"That's fucking weird," I mutter, retrieving the keys out of my pocket as I reach my car. Dylan and I talk about once a week, but usually, if I miss his call, he doesn't call back until a few days later. But today he's tried to call over eight times and sent one text.

Dylan: Call me ASAP.

I dial his number as I hop into my car and turn the engine on, cranking up the heater with the phone pressed to my ear.

"Hey," Dylan answers with an edge to his voice. "I was actually going to try to call you again."

45

"Yeah, I was at work," I reply, staring out the window. "What's up?"

"Nothing... well, everything." He hesitates then sighs. "It's about Tyler."

My heart rate quickens at the mention of my other brother's name. "What happened to him?"

Dylan sighs again, and it's more weighted this time. "I got a call from him a few days ago, and he said that he needed help, that he's been living on the streets. I could tell he was ripped out of his mind—I could barely understand half the words he said."

"Living on the streets where exactly?"

"I'm not sure yet. I haven't gotten that far with him." When he sighs for the third time, I know it's bad. Whatever's going on, it's really, really bad. "He was actually headed up to Virginia when he called me. I guess he found out where I lived and started hitchhiking to my place. He was strung out, and we're trying to help him detox right now, but I'm not sure how well it's going to work."

"Where was he hitchhiking from?" I dare to ask, wondering if it's from wherever my parents are.

What if it is?

What does that mean?

That they'll be entering Dylan's life again too?

Will he let them?

A thousand questions race through my mind as Dylan says, "I have no idea. Somewhere down south, I think, but he acts like he doesn't remember."

I grip onto the steering wheel, attempting to control the frustration stirring inside me. But I've never been great at controlling my emotions, and I start to sweat from the anxiousness I'm feeling. "Or maybe he does remember," I say tightly. "But he's not saying anything because Mom and Dad told him not to."

"Yeah, I kind of wondered the same thing. Been wondering it for the few months after you got ahold of me and told me what'd been going on. But then again, Tyler is, well, Tyler, and he might have been living on the streets so fucking high he really can't remember where he was."

"Yeah, I guess so."

Dylan's probably right. Tyler could have easily just wandered in from off the streets, but part of me wants it to be the other way around, wants him to know where my parents are. I don't know why I feel that way. It's not like I want them back in my life. I don't even want to see them again unless it's because my dad is behind bars, just like his father—my grandfather—is now.

"I know what you're thinking," Dylan says, interrupting my thoughts. "And you need to stop thinking about that. You need to try to let it go. Don't worry about Mom and Dad anymore."

"I'm not worrying about them," I lie and really well too. I've always been good at lying, which isn't a good thing, but it's something I've had to learn how to do from an early age when people would ask about my bruises and broken bones.

"Well, I didn't really mean worry. More like, let them get to you."

"I'm fine. Really," I lie again because I don't feel fine. I feel angry. All the time.

"Are you still seeing your therapist?" Dylan asks cautiously.

"Yeah." I turn down the heater. "Once a week, every week."

"Good. I think it's good for you. I still see mine sometimes when things get really bad, like the other day when I had to pick up Tyler." When I don't say anything, uncertain of what to say, Dylan changes the subject. "But anyway, I just wanted to call and let you know what's up. We might check Tyler into a rehab if we can get him to commit, so he might be around for Thanksgiving when you come out here."

I frown. "Thanksgiving?"

"Yeah, you're coming up, right? I mean, I thought that's what you said."

What I said was I'd think about it, but I still mutter, "Yeah, I guess so."

My lungs begin to constrict as I think about what happened at Thanksgiving. It'd started out okay, spending time with Callie. I'd ended up having sex with her and even though it wasn't my first time, it was the most intense experience of my life at the time. But then things had gotten ugly and the beautiful moment was tainted by reality.

"Look, I've got to go. My breaks over," I lie to Dylan for the third time during this conversation. "But let me know what happens with Tyler."

"I will." He hesitates as I shut off the engine and get out of the car. "Kayden, just so you know, he's been asking about you—what you're doing, if you're okay. He keeps saying he wants to talk to you, but I'm not going to let him until he sobers up, just to make sure he doesn't say… Well, anything that isn't meant to be said." I think he might be trying to protect me, but I'm not sure since no one has ever done that for me before, at least no one in my family. "And you only have to talk to him if you want to."

I don't know how to respond. Dylan and I have been getting along okay, but right now, he's showing quite a bit of emotion directed toward me. It's strange and unfamiliar,

49

especially since I spent a lot of time thinking that he hated me after he took off when he was eighteen and left me with our dad and mom, never so much as calling to say where he was living. It's something we haven't really talked about too much, although my therapist thinks it might be healthy for us to do so. However, I don't want to go down that road yet—open up those old scars that are still trying to heal.

"Okay… thanks for letting me know," I say awkwardly as I lock the car door then shut it because it's too old school for a key fob.

"Yeah, no problem," Dylan replies, sounding uncomfortable himself. I hear someone say something in the background and he quickly adds, "Oh, and Liz wants to know if you're bringing anyone here for Thanksgiving with you."

I want to tell him I haven't even fully committed to coming yet, but instead say, "I'm not sure, but I'll let you know soon."

"Okay, but just so you know, we'd love to have you and Callie here if she can come."

Again, I'm a little thrown off by this weird I-care-for-you thing he's got going. I keep my composure, though, and say good-bye before heading back to work, even though I have ten more minutes of break time. I try not to think about Tyler too much, yet I can't help it. Because what if he really does know.

Where my father is.

Chapter 5

#134 Invite Someone to Prom **coughs** aka Halloween Party/Concert.

Callie

"Really?" I say to Seth as I read what he just wrote on my whiteboard. Seth and I have been creating a to-do list since the beginning of freshman year when we first became friends. There's no rule for what goes on there. It simply needs to be something we think at least one of us needs to try. This whiteboard version actually starts at one-hundred since the list got so long that we had to transfer some of them onto a piece of paper.

"Yes, really." Seth taps the marker against number one hundred seventeen. "It isn't any weirder than this one."

"Hey, I totally did that the other day." I snatch the marker from his hand and draw a line through number one-hundred seventeen.

"You're so weird," he says as I put the cap of the marker back on and toss it on my bed.

I roll my eyes at him. "That's the pot calling the kettle

black."

"Totally," he agrees, his gaze drifting to the window. "So are you ready for this?"

My face bunches up in confusion. "Ready for what?"

He taps his finger against the whiteboard right where he just wrote one-hundred thirty-four. "Duh, what you're going to do today."

Shaking my head, I sink down on the bed. "I'm not doing that."

He puts his hands on his hips and stares me down. "You so are."

I fold my arms and aim him a challenging look. "Am not."

"You have to," he insists. "The concert is tomorrow, and I already told Greyson you were coming."

"Fine, I'll ask Kayden," I tell him, defeated. "But not in some weird, cheesy prom way like people do in high school."

"No way. You so are, Callie Lawrence." He grabs my arm and jerks me to my feet so hard I stumble. "This is something you seriously need to do."

I give him the nastiest look ever. I get that he thinks I need to relive my high school days since they sucked big time, and I want to, but at the same time... "I'm afraid I'll be living in the past if I do it."

His determination softens, but he still pulls me toward the door, throwing my coat at me in the process. "Nope. Not at all." He opens the door and leads me out into the hallway, navigating us around a group of people loitering in the hallways. "See, this is you and I walking away from the past and heading to the future."

"You're speaking metaphorically, aren't you?" I ask as we reach the elevator and he presses the down button.

"I had my Philosophy class today," he admits as the elevator doors swing open and we step inside. "Now, would you pretty please do this with me?" His finger hovers over the button to the bottom floor, waiting for me to agree because, in the end, regardless of how pushy he is, he'll always back down if I ask him to. That's the thing with Seth and why he's such a good friend.

"Oh, fine. Let's go be cheesy," I huff as if I'm aggravated, but in the end, we're both smiling. And really, that's kind of the point of it—of anything—isn't it?

"So this is what people do when they ask each other to prom, huh?" I stare at the front of Kayden's lofty dorm building as Seth snaps a thin branch from the tree, causing a pile of snow to fall on his head.

Sweeping the snow out of his hair, he nods then

crouches down and draws a heart in the snow. "Yes, you have to be creative with these things. In fact, the more creative you are, the better." As he says it, he writes in the snow: *Kayden, will you go to a Halloween concert with me? I would swoon over the moon if you did.* Then he stands up with a proud expression. "See, now all you have to do is go get him." He drops the branch and dusts the snow off his gloves.

"Swoon over the moon?" I question, and he gives me a *what* look. I retrieve my gloves from my pocket and slip my fingers inside them. "I have a better idea." I pick up the branch and brush my hands across the surface of the snow, erasing what he wrote and giggling when he starts to complain. Then I kneel down and write something that's actually from me.

"If I'm going to do this, then I should do it," I tell him as I trace the tip of the tree branch across the snow. When I'm done, I stand up and admire my handiwork.

Seth steps beside me and reads what I wrote. "*Kayden, let me dazzle you at a Halloween concert. P.S. Seth made me do this because he put it on the list.*" He gives me a look. "That's really what you want to write?"

"Yep, I think it's perfect."

He sighs, but he's smiling, so I know he thinks I'm amusing. "Here, let me see your phone."

I reach into my pocket and give my phone to him, not really thinking too much about it. "Where's yours?"

He's chuckling under his breath as he types something. "In my pocket."

"Then why do you need mine?"

Laughing, he tosses me my phone back. "Let me know how it goes and if you need a ride later." He saunters off toward the parking lot.

"Seth, what did you do?" I shout at him, but then shake my head and go into my text messages to see for myself. "*Hey, lover. Meet me outside your dorm building in ten. I have a naughty little surprise for you,*" I read it aloud, unsure whether to be angry or amused. I decide to go for the latter since Seth didn't mean anything by it and Kayden shouldn't think much of it. At least, I hope he doesn't... or maybe I do.

Kayden: Hmm... I'm intrigued. I'll be down in a sec.

Sighing, I put my phone away and wait for him to come out to me. I wonder if he thinks I'm going to bombard him with another question like I did the other day. I've kind of been making it a habit lately, texting him to meet me out here in the middle of the yard that looks like a frozen tundra.

I should really find another way to do stuff like this.

A couple of minutes later, Kayden walks outside, stuffing his hands into the pockets of his coat. The wind blows through his brown hair that hangs in his eyes and flips up at his ears. His shoulders are strong, his entire body lean and in shape, but his flesh is covered in scars, put there by both himself and his father. Still, he's absolutely gorgeous. I've always thought so, even when we were younger. Our parents actually knew each other—small town thing—and had a lot of parties that we attended, but Kayden never really noticed me until I stepped in one time right after graduation when his father was in the middle of hitting him. It was back when I was still cutting my own hair and wore clothes two sizes too big so I wouldn't get noticed by anyone.

But that night, he noticed me, like I had always noticed him.

And I—neither of us—were the same again.

"You know you can come up to my room, right?" Kayden teases as he strolls up to me. "There's not a 'no girls allowed' rule." He winks at me as he stops in front of me, all smiles. But I can see in his eyes that he's keeping something from me—something that's bothering him. It's not the same sadness I've been seeing for a few weeks. This is different. He's carrying more weight around, like when we first were together and I didn't know about his

57

problems. "So what's the naughty thing you wanted to show me?" His gaze skims down my body and makes my skin feel like it's on fire.

"Yeah… sorry about that," I say with an exaggerated sigh. "Seth actually sent you that text."

He chuckles under his breath. "I was kind of wondering." He looks around at the trees and the parking lot. "Where is he?"

"Oh, he left," I tell him. His eyes land back on me and he waits for me to explain, so I step back and let him read my little snowflake note.

At first, he appears puzzled, but then he starts to laugh. "You two are so weird."

"Yeah, I know…" I trail off, wishing I wasn't nervous. "The thing starts at eight. We can go there or meet up because I know you have practice and stuff."

He looks back up at me and places his hands on my hips. "I'd love to go with you, but we'll have to meet there if that's okay? I can't miss practice or coach will fucking flip out."

My anxiousness alleviates. "That's perfectly okay. And thank you for going with me. And sorry about the weird note. Seth just thought since I never got to go to prom, this kind of thing would be fun, but now that I think about it, it's kind of weird." I stop rambling. I don't know why, but I feel stupidly high right now. It's not like we haven't been on dates before—we've been on a ton of them—but this time, I'll get to wear the dress I bought. If someone had asked me a year ago if I ever thought I'd be excited about doing such a thing, I'd have told them no. But here I am, spreading my wings and flying all on my own.

Kayden looks at me sympathetically. "Callie, I'm so sorry... that you didn't get to do that stuff."

"It's not your fault. And besides, you're helping me do that stuff now."

"Good I'm glad. It feels like I am." He gives me a sad smile, which I don't like. He's feeling sorry for me, and I don't want him to.

"Kayden, it's fine—I'm fine," I promise him. "What happened... it's in the past, and I'm working on moving on—moving forward."

He looks even sadder, but I'm not sure if it has to do with me anymore. "Moving forward is good." He clears his throat then shakes off whatever he's feeling. "Do I have to dress up, though? For the party?"

I shake my head. "Not if you don't want to."

"Are you going to?"

"Yes."

He momentarily considers something. "I'll see what I

can come up with."

"Seth wanted you to wear tights," I tell him, playfully pinching his side. "And be Peter Pan."

He swiftly shakes his head. "No way in hell am I doing that."

"It's okay," I assure him. "I didn't want to be Tinkerbell, anyway."

He nudges his foot with mine, his sad mood lightening. "What are you going to be?"

I wink at him, trying to be suave. I think it comes off more awkward than anything, but his laugh makes it worth it. "It's a surprise."

His eyes search mine, and I think he's going to say something deeply profound, like maybe what's got him all down, but then he decides against it. "You want to come inside? I have Doritos, Coke, and we can stream Netflix."

"Awe, you know the way to my heart." As my grin breaks through, everything feels perfect for a moment. If only Kayden could feel the same way too. But the hint of sadness in his eyes tells me that he doesn't.

Chapter 6

#115 Share a Passionate Dorito/Coke Kiss.

Kayden

I'm the shittiest boyfriend in the history of boyfriends. Seriously. Callie is always putting her heart out there for me, and I can't even tell her about the call I got from Dylan today. I don't even know why I can't tell her about it. Or maybe I do. Maybe I know that Callie will make me talk about it because that's the kind of person she is, and I really don't want to talk about it.

After I agree to go to the party/concert with her, we go up to my room. I feel like the biggest douche after her whole statement about prom. I went to every one of mine, did all that stupid shit in high school that was supposed to mean something, but I took it for granted. And here Callie is, trying to make up for everything she missed out on by going to a Halloween concert. I need to start doing more things for her, making her feel more special, stop being such a shitty boyfriend.

Once we settle on my bed with my laptop in front of

us, we pick out a movie, and then binge on snacks and drinks. My roommate is gone so we have the place to ourselves, which usually I'd take advantage of by exploring every inch of Callie's body, but today my head's in a weird place.

Callie must sense my distance, too—of course she does—because about halfway through the movie, she moves out of my arms and pauses the screen. "Okay, what's up?" She grabs a handful of chips and dumps them into her mouth.

"Nothing's up," I lie, glad the lamp is the only lighting so she can't see my face clearly.

She takes a sip of her soda, eyeing me the entire time. "You know I can tell when you're lying, right?"

I sit up on the bed and rest back against the headboard. "How?"

When she leans over me to set the soda on the nightstand, I breathe in the scent of her hair; strawberries with a hint of vanilla. "Because your jaw twitches when you're not being honest."

My fingers absentmindedly travel to my jawline. "It does not."

She bites on her lip to keep from grinning. "Does too."

I shake my head as I stretch out my legs. "Then why

62

haven't you mentioned it before?"

"Because you'd try to control it, and I wouldn't have my little secret lie detector anymore," she says, hitching a leg over me and straddling my lap. "But I'm calling you out now because I want the truth." She places her hands on my chest and lowers her body toward mine, looking directly into my eyes. "What's bothering you?"

I'm overwhelmed by her nearness and her intensity. Even after almost a year of being with her, it still gets under my skin in the best way possible. My head becomes foggy, and I find myself divulging without even meaning to.

"I got a call from Dylan today."

Her legs tighten around me as her muscles tense. "I know he calls you sometimes, but by your tone... I'm guessing it wasn't a normal checking-in call."

I nod, knowing I have to tell her what happened now, otherwise I'd be really lying instead of just keeping things to myself. "It wasn't. He called to tell me that"—I clutch onto her hips because touching her makes everything easier—"he found Tyler. Or, well, Tyler found him, I guess."

"What do you mean found? Where was he?"

I shrug. "Dylan's not sure yet. Tyler was high when Dylan found him... I guess Tyler's been living on the street or something..." I trail off, still unsure if I believe that story.

"What? You think Tyler might have been living somewhere else and is lying about it?" Callie asks, reading me like an open book.

I shrug again. "I'm not sure, but maybe." I don't want to talk about this anymore, and I think Callie can tell.

"What can I do to make it better?" She puts her palm on my cheek and smooths her thumb along my jawline.

My fingers slip under the bottom of her shirt and caress her soft flesh. "I can think of a few things."

A gasp escapes her lips as my fingers drift up her shirt toward her breasts. It's the little noises she makes every time we're together that drive me crazier than anything else. They're what make the moment over quicker than I want because I can't keep myself under control. Just like now.

Tangling my fingers through her hair, I tip her head back and bring her in for a passionate Dorito/Coke tasting kiss.

"Kayden," she groans, her fingers tensing for the briefest moment on my chest, right where my heart is throbbing. I know she can feel it, feel what she does to me, and I hope it lets her understand what she means to me.

As my fingers slide beneath her bra and graze her nipple, she instantly surrenders into my arms, opening her mouth and allowing me to deepen the kiss as she rolls her hips against mine. Now I'm the one who's groaning while tugging at her hair, nipping at her lips, biting her neck, licking her collarbone. I'm being a little rougher with her than I normally am, but I'll stop the moment she utters the word.

She never does, though, instead breaking the kiss to grab the bottom of my shirt and tug it over my head. Then her fingers find the scars on my chest, and I struggle to breathe as she traces the rough and jagged patterns of each one. Her lips follow the path her fingers make, planting kisses on my skin. Callie knows where my scars came from, knows that some I put there myself, while others my father gave me. I haven't given her every gory detail of what happened, though, wanting to spare her the ugliness of them.

After Callie is done kissing pretty much every inch of my chest, she reclines back and lifts her arms above her head so I can remove her shirt. I love that she trusts me enough to do this without so much as tensing anymore.

Once her shirt comes off, I unclasp her bra and my mouth promptly closes over her nipple. She lets out this gasp mixed with a delirious plea as her fingers slide through my hair, tugging at the roots, both pulling me and pushing me closer. Her legs clamp down at my sides as she rocks her hips again, causing a throaty groan to escape my mouth and I just about lose it right then and there.

Not being able to stand the little amount of clothing left on our bodies any longer, I move away from her to yank her jeans and panties off. Then she helps me with the button of my pants and I slip out of then. She's on the pill now, so I don't have to get a condom out of my pocket like I used to, which is a really good thing because there's been a lot of times where we've gotten so caught up in the moment we almost forget about protection.

After I discard my boxers, I lie her down on her back and cover her body with mine. She's practically panting as she arches her hips and grabs at my ass so I can slide easily inside her. But I move almost painfully slow just to see that look on her face, the one I've seen many times whenever her eyes glaze over and she gets lost.

She moans as she clutches onto my shoulders, stabbing at my flesh, grasping onto me while she drifts away and lets go. And there's nothing left to do except join her, wishing this is how things could always be.

Just her and I and nothing else.

Chapter 7

#116 Hang On.

Kayden

After the night I spent with Callie, it feels like things are going to be okay. That maybe I can let all this shit go and not worry about it. That maybe I'll never get resolution for what happened to me and I just need to move on.

It's morning, and I'm hanging out in my room, trying to catch up on some assignments, when my phone starts to ring. I cringe when I see Dylan's name on the screen, instantly thinking the phone call is going to be bad.

I almost don't answer it, but knowing it'll drive me mad if I don't, I make myself reach for the phone and press talk. Niko is hanging out at the computer desk, playing a game so I head out into the hallway.

"What's up?" I ask Dylan as I shut the door behind me. I'm figuring it's a call about Tyler, so when he says, "It's about dad," my brain almost doesn't register it.

"Huh…? What…? Did you…?" I'm struck speechless.

"Kayden, I'm so sorry. Maybe I shouldn't be telling

you this," Dylan says, which is seeming to become his M.O. lately.

I make a right toward the bathrooms, maneuvering through people, practically shoving them out of my way. "Telling me what? Because I seriously didn't hear anything but it's about dad."

"I found Mom and Dad, Kayden... and it's bad... Well, bad depending on how you look at it." There's his sigh again.

I make it to the bathroom and lock myself in a stall. "How so?" I slump against the stall door, telling myself to breathe, but my heart is taking up all the fucking space in my chest. It's like I've been kicked in the gut and slammed in the face over and over again as Dylan's words replay in my mind.

I found Mom and Dad.

"Dad's in the hospital." When he pauses, I can tell he's struggling to keep his voice balanced. "I didn't get too much information, considering Mom is the queen of lying about shit she doesn't want to talk about." Another pause. "Are you okay?"

I take a deep breath. Then another. And another.

"Yeah..."

I found Mom and Dad.

"Kayden?"

Dad's in the hospital.

Is this my resolution?

"I have to go," I choke then hang up the phone. My pulse is pounding, my skin dampening with sweat, and I can't get air into my lungs. It's been a while since I've felt this bad but I can't help it. The thoughts going through my head… I've wanted resolution, but not like this.

Or did I?

Am I that kind of a person?

To wish pain upon someone else?

Am I like my father?

The last thought is fucking horrifying. I feel like I'm about to fall again, tumble in into the dark, pick up that blade and slice away until whatever's inside me bleeds out. I don't want to do it, but at the same time I do.

I want it.

Want it.

Want it.

I'm barely able to hang on.

Chapter 8
#122 Dance Like it's Your Prom.

Callie

Once upon a time, there was a girl who thought she was a princess, and really, weren't all girls supposed to be?

She grew up happy with a loving, perhaps overly doting mother and a father who took care of her. Her older brother wasn't too bad for the most part, as much as any older brother was. And while she didn't grow up in a castle centered in the knolls of grassland country, blossoming with flowers and trees, her simple home felt like a palace in her small town. It made her feel protected and safe from all the bad she'd heard whispers of yet wasn't sure existed since she'd never seen any of it for herself.

Yes, all was well in the princess's world. Then on her twelfth birthday that all changed when the bad entered the walls of her palace. He didn't break down the place or force his way inside like how it occurred in books or movies. He simply walked through the door with welcomed arms. He didn't have fangs or sharp teeth that would warn the princess that maybe he wasn't good but a monster. No, he was dressed in normal clothes, had normal teeth, and he even had a normal smile. He was simply a normal guy. At least, that was what the princess thought.

But the princess was wrong, and she soon and very tragically found out what the bad things were that she'd only heard whispers about.

In a house full of balloons and presents, the guy trapped her in a place she'd once felt safe in and broke the princess into a thousand pieces that would never fully be found again. And he didn't just break them, but he stole some of them, keeping them hidden where no one else could see them.

After it was all over, the broken princess was no more. She felt like a girl who simply was invisible. Princesses were supposed to be happy, pretty, have lots of friends, and go to parties, not be so broken. But the girl no longer did or felt any of those things. Her palace was now a prison. And the family that had once brought her happiness felt like nothing more than ghosts in a dark and unfamiliar world she'd been forced into.

Invisible vines grew around the home, full of thorns, making it painful to both leave and stay. Nowhere felt safe. And that was how she believed things would always be, that

71

she would suffer from the bad, all alone, for the rest of her life.

However, six years later, on a warm, summer night, the girl discovered she wasn't the only one being broken by bad, scary monsters. They were everywhere, destroying walls and people—destroying one guy in particular. He wasn't just a guy, though. He was also the most beautiful and broken guy the girl had ever seen. She knew the moment she saw him she had to save him from the monster that stood before him with his fangs out...

"Whatcha doing?" Seth asks as he strolls into my room without knocking. He's dressed head to toe in black with studs on his belt and an array of leather bands on his wrists. His boots are clunky and his jacket with buckles is trendy.

I'm not even sure what he's supposed to be. We just sort of wandered into this gothic store and started picking out articles of clothing that weren't in the norm for us and the outfit he has on was what he'd ended up with.

"Because that's what Halloween is supposed to be about, right?" Seth had said at the store. "It's all about being someone different."

I'd agreed and we'd actually taken Violet, Luke's girlfriend, to pick out her costume at the same store a day later. Although hers was a lot different from mine, and honestly,

Violet looked like she belonged in the store.

I blink my thoughts away from Halloween outfits and focus on answering Seth's question. "I'm writing a nontraditional fairytale for my portfolio."

He peers over my shoulder and reads a few sentences on the screen. "I have a feeling from the title that this happy introduction is going to go dark." He pauses, looking at me. "Are you writing a story about yourself?"

I shake my head and close the laptop, feeling self-conscious. "No, just writing about stuff I know."

He raises his eyebrows in skepticism. "You know, you're brave if you tell your story."

I set the laptop on the nightstand. "But it's not my story. It's for a class assignment. Nothing more, nothing less."

"Hmmm…" He's not buying it, but he drops the subject anyway, which is good because his accusation is making me the slightest bit uncomfortable. "So you about ready for tonight?"

I nod as I cross the room and throw open the closet door. "Yeah, should I get dressed now though? Or take the dress with me and change somewhere else?" I grab the hanger with the dress on it and step back into the room. "I'm not sure if I should wander around dressed like this."

Seth rolls his eyes at me. "Oh, my darling Callie, it's Halloween. You could walk around naked and people

73

wouldn't think too much of it."

My cheeks start to heat. "Well, I'm not going to do that."

"Yeah, we can leave that to me." He waggles his eyebrows and he has a teasing glint in his eyes that makes me giggle.

"Fine, I'll put the dress on now." I step back into the closest and slip out of my pants and T-shirt. "So what's Greyson dressed up as?"

"His normal, adorable self," Seth answers.

"He didn't want to dress up?" I slip the dress off the hanger and hesitate, deciding if I really want to wear this. Yeah, it's just a dress, but it's shorter than the few I've worn over the last few months. It's gorgeous, though—dark blue with studded black lines that run vertically and horizontally in the chest area. To go with it, I have a pair of knee-high lacy stockings, black knee-high boots, and a velvet choker. When I bought it, I had this image of a gothic rocker chick, totally unlike the usual stuff I wear.

Deciding that I need to do this, I get dressed then twist my hair up, leaving a few stray strands down to frame my face. Even though my jacket doesn't really go with it, I still grab it from the hanger, knowing I'm going to freeze to death without it.

"Ta-da!" I exclaim as I spring out of the closet with my hands up, striking a pose.

Seth is messing around with his phone, but when he glances up, his jaw drops. "Holy shit, you look hot."

I instantly wrap my arms around myself. "Maybe I should change."

Shaking his head, his eyes scroll up my attire. "No way. You are staying just like that." He waltzes up to me, reaching into his jacket pocket. "And I have two more things to add to make you look even sexier."

"Seth," I hiss because his compliments are embarrassing me, "stop saying stuff like that."

When he takes his hand out of his pocket, he has two items in his palm—a tube of lipstick and eyeliner. "Well, you better get used to it because you're going to hear stuff like that a lot tonight, especially from Kayden." He grins as he pats the desk chair. "Now sit down and put this stuff on."

I take the dark red lipstick and the kohl eyeliner. "Where did you get this stuff?"

He shrugs as he hands me my compact and then sits down on the bed. "I borrowed it from Violet."

I click open the compact and set it on the desk. "Did you ask or just take it?"

"I told her what it was for," he says, motioning at me

to get a move on. "Now would you hurry your beautiful ass up? We're going to be late."

I lean over and begin to apply the liner. "Violet really didn't mind that it was for me?"

"No, it was the least she could do after you helped her with kickboxing and costume shopping today," he says as I apply the lipstick.

I rub my lips together as I put the cap on. "She doesn't owe me anything, Seth. I was glad to help her."

"I know, but she didn't mind. Besides, I think, even though she won't admit it, she likes having friends."

"Yeah, maybe." Although, I think there's way more to it than that. When I first met Violet, I thought she was mean. And honestly, I was under the impression that she might have been a prostitute. But now, after getting to know her and seeing the stuff on the news about her parents' deaths, I think Violet has even more problems than I do.

I hand Seth back the makeup then slip my jacket on, wishing Kayden could have drove with me instead of meeting us there, but I understand he's busy with practice and stuff.

Seth must sense some sort of weird vibe from me because he links his arm through mine and tugs me out the door. It's pretty quiet on the elevator ride down, yet once we reach the bottom, all bets are off.

"So this is how the youngins celebrate Halloween, huh?" I ask, my eyes wide as I take in the lounge area packed with people dressed up in so many different types of costumes that it's madness. Everything from ghosts to slutty nurses to some sort of strange looking zucchini costume is present. Music is playing and people are chatting and laughing and some are even running around and screaming as they drink from plastic cups I'm sure aren't filled with punch. Where the RA is, I have no clue, but I'm guessing nowhere within a mile radius since I'm pretty certain the noise can be heard from that far away.

"Wait until we get to the concert," Seth promises, noting my shocked stare.

"I've never been to a concert," I admit as we turn for the exit and step outside into the frigid breeze. The ground is frozen, making the heeled boots I'm wearing complicated to walk in. The sun has set, the moon and stars bright in the sky and twinkling right along with all the orange, black, and purple lights around the area.

"I know you haven't." Seth steers us toward the grass, which is covered by a thin layer of snow, and we start to make our way to the parking lot. "I promise, you're going to love it. In fact, I think..." He trails off at the sight of a figure crossing the grass and heading in our direction. It takes me a moment or two to realize who it is.

"Hey, what are you doing there?" I ask, releasing Seth's arm and meeting Kayden halfway. "I thought you had practice."

He doesn't answer until he reaches me. "I know. I left early... I wanted to pick you up." He tugs at the bottom of his sleeves, seeming both nervous and excited.

I throw my arms around him and hug him. "You didn't have to do that."

He looks amazing tonight in his black and grey plaid shirt that's unbuttoned enough so I can see the fitted black T-shirt he's wearing that shows off his muscular abs. It's topped off with a leather jacket, black jeans, and boots, and his brown hair is just the slightest bit messy in the sexiest way possible. Not really a Halloween costume, but totally not in his norm, and it makes him even more ridiculously good looking than he already is.

"I know I didn't." He kisses my temple then pulls back to look me in the eye. "But I wanted to." He opens his mouth to say something else, but then his gaze drifts down my attire. I'm still holding the jacket, even though it's freezing, so he gets the full view of me.

"Holy shit," he breathes, his arms falling to his sides.

He scratches at his wrist, his eyes drinking me in. "You look—"

"Don't say hot or sexy," Seth warns, strolling up to us. "She seems to take those a bit offensively."

The corners of Kayden's mouth quirk. "I was actually going to say beautiful."

"Liar," Seth coughs, but then grins.

Repressing a smile, Kayden lifts one of his arms toward me. The first thing I notice is that there's something sticking out of the sleeve of his shirt... a piece of gauze maybe. But then my eyes travel to what's in his hand. A rose with a short, bare stem. He takes it and tucks in my hair beside my ear, making me feel pretty. I've never been a fan of looking this way. That is, until now. But I think that has more to do with the way Kayden is looking at me with a lustful, heated, burning desire.

Screw prom.

This is so, so much better.

I'm about to tell him how much I love him when my attention darts to a pale figure running across the grass, yelling, "WOO HOO! Halloween fucking rocks!"

He looks familiar, and I squint to get a better look at what's going on. "Wait. Is he...?" I trail off when I realize the reason why the figure is so pale. "He's *naked*!"

Kayden's eyes widen as he tracks my gaze, then he

places his hand over my eyes. "What the hell is with streakers and Halloween? I swear I see at least one a year."

Seth chuckles. "It's the freedom in the air to be whoever you want to be."

"I'm pretty sure he's in my English class," I say. "And I don't think I'll ever be able to look him in the eye again."

"Why?" Seth asks. "You're not the one who was seen in a very unflattering outfit. You should hold your head up high, baby girl."

"I know, but every time I look at him, I'll picture his…" I bite down on my lip, unable to finish the sentence, let alone get the picture of what I just witnessed out of my head.

This time, Kayden laughs and lowers his hand from my eyes. "You're so adorable." Then he kisses me, and I don't feel shy or ashamed. Adorable I can handle. Kayden kissing me I can handle. Seeing more naked people tonight, I'm not so sure.

The night is turning out to be amazing. The atmosphere is electric, the décor is vibrant in the most eerie way possible, and the rock combined orchestra music the band is playing is hauntingly poetic to the point that it gives me chills. Violet calls it Symphonic Rock.

We've been dancing for a while—Seth, Greyson, Violet, and I. Kayden and Luke are hanging out at the table. Luke seems distracted by something and Kayden keeps getting texts from someone, so they're both living in their own world. It makes me a little sad that Kayden's not out here with me, but I don't have time to wallow when Violet decides she's going to teach me to dance per Seth's suggestion.

"There's no way I can dance like her," I tell the both of them, not because I'm afraid, but because I really don't think I can. Violet dances in the most beautiful way ever, like a mix between a ballerina and one of those rocker chicks that can head bang. She seriously looks like she belongs on stage with a microphone in her hand, a band of guitars and violins playing in the background.

"Sure you can," Violet says with an encouraging smile that looks foreign on her because she hardly ever does it. She seems in a good mood tonight, though, so I decide to play along and follow her lead.

"Now, move your hips," Violet instructs, putting her hand on my waist and guiding me to the rhythm.

I'm not one for my personal space getting invaded, but I shake it off and try to do what she says since we're standing in the center of a crammed crowd already.

"Let the music own you," she says. "Don't overthink

it."

"And dance like you mean it!" Seth shouts over the music as he raises his hands in the air.

I take a deep inhale and try to do what they both said, but I've never been one for dancing.

"You're overthinking it," Seth tells me, his eyes wandering over my shoulders. "And now you have the perfect distraction." My brows furrow as he mouths, *Dance like it's your prom.*

All I can picture when he says it is what I've seen on movies. Bad music and decorations, while people way too overdressed rock back and forth with their hands on each other or while they do some sort of silly dance off. Then Kayden comes up to me, takes my hand, and spins me around, causing laughter to erupt from my lips.

"Awe, and the secret dance moves come out," I say, laughing when he spins me again and then crashes me against his chest. Kayden once told me that he secretly knew how to dance because his mother used him as a dance partner when he was younger.

His arms slide around me as I rest my head on his shoulder. "That was supposed to be a secret," he whispers in my ear, giving my lobe a soft nip.

The band takes a break and the DJ turns on a song I

know, "My Immortal" by Evanescence. It's slow and relaxing, and I find myself unstiffening and leaning against Kayden as I rock to the music and drift away from reality.

"I hope you're having fun tonight," he whispers in my ear, his hand that's on the small of my back pushing me closer. There's something in his touch—a desperation.

"Of course I am." My eyelids slip shut as the warmth of his body drowns me, and I pull him closer, wishing he knew that everything was going to be okay. If only I could make him see that, somehow. See that he'll always have me. That he'll never be alone.

"Good. That's all I want for you—nothing but fun." His breath catches. "You deserve to be happy."

I angle my chin up to look him in the eye. "I am happy." *Unlike him.* He looks like he's in pain, on the verge of crying. "Who was texting you tonight?"

He shuts his eyes and shakes his head. "I don't want to talk about it… don't want to make another one of your nights depressing."

Where the heck is this coming from?

"You don't make any of my nights depressing. What the fuck, Kayden? Where is this coming from?" It's rare for me to curse, so when I do, it has a purpose. Right now, I'm panicking because he looks like a guy who's about to break up with his girlfriend. "A-are you b-breaking up with me?"

His eyes snap wide in horror. "What? No! Why the hell would you say that?"

"Because you look like you're about to!"

"I would never say that to you! Ever!"

We're yelling over the music, and I hate it. We never yell, even behind closed doors, only talk passionately. Yet this is yelling, and it's giving me the worst feeling in the world.

As if he suddenly just realizes we're in a crowded place, he lowers his voice as he takes my hand. "Will you come with me? I have something..." He exhales loudly and runs his free hand through his hair. "I have something I need to talk to you about."

Swallowing the lump in my throat, I nod then follow him off the dance floor, waving to Seth on my way. Seth gives me a concerned look and then puts his finger and thumb up to the side of his face like a phone. I nod, understanding he wants me to call him later. Then I turn and focus on my steps because that's easier than focusing on what the hell just caused Kayden and me to yell at each other for the first time.

After we collect our jackets from the coat check, we step outside into the nipping air. I instantly slip my jacket on and zip it up, shivering as Kayden leads me to his car.

He opens the passenger door for me without saying a word then rounds the car and gets in himself. Then he starts the engine and turns the heat on, before staring out the window, gripping the steering wheel so firmly his hands begin to tremble.

"I fucked up," he finally says, withdrawing his hands from the wheel and wiping his palms on his jeans.

I'm about to ask him what he messed up with, but he rolls up the sleeve of his shirt and shows me the answer. Earlier, when he'd picked me up, I thought I'd noticed a piece of gauze sticking out of his shirt, but I'd stupidly gotten sidetracked by the rose and naked man and completely forgotten to ask him about it.

God, I should have asked him.

"What happened?" I whisper, even though I sadly know the answer.

He shuts his eyes and rubs his hand down his face, releasing a weighted breath. "I was feeling a lot of pressure lately, and instead of dealing with it, I let it eat away at me. Then some shit happened today... and I... I sort of just lost it." He opens his eyes, but looks ahead instead of at me. "That's why I was able to pick you up today. I had to miss practice so I could go talk to my therapist."

I know therapy is good for him, and I'm glad he does it, but still, sometimes I wish he'd talk to me about stuff.

"What was the stuff that happened today? Or do you not want to talk about it?"

He rubs his hand down his face again, this time so roughly I'm worried he's doing it to cause physical pain to himself. "I should have talked to you to begin with instead of doing what I did. The therapist says it happens, though. Relapses happen." He squeezes his eyes shut, but a tear or two slip out.

I'm not sure what to do or say, if there's anything I can do or say since I don't know what this is about. I know enough to know his cutting comes from when he doesn't want to feel emotional pain, but what caused him emotional pain?

I'm about to ask him, try to get him to talk to me again, but this time he gives me the answer without me having to ask.

His eyes open, and he looks at me, not bothering to hide the tears. "Dylan found my mother and father."

Chapter 9
#145 Fall in Love with the Same Person Again.

Kayden

I've always been good at pretending. I pretended my father wasn't an abusive asshole for eighteen years of my life. That my mother wasn't a sedated zombie for the same amount of time. For twelve years, I pretended that I didn't cut myself because physical pain was easier than emotional pain. Pretending in front of Callie has always been difficult, though. She's not so easily persuaded to believe things she knows aren't real just because it's easier to deal with than the ugly truth.

Callie always wants the truth, no matter how raw and painful it is. And I need to learn how to give the truth to her, which is something my therapist and I talked about today after I went in for an emergency visit.

It was Dylan's call that set me off, but it was the emotions that surfaced afterward that set me over the edge. Anger. Hurt. Blinding rage. Relief. Guilt over the relief. It ate away at my soul and heart, and even though I fought to hang on, I slipped up and let a razor eat away at my flesh and blood. But when I was finished I felt guilty for doing it so I sought help, which is better than what I used to do. And it's helping me get through the texts Dylan's been sending me of updates about my parents.

And now I'm seeking Callie, even though I'm scared shitless to put myself out there.

"What do you mean Dylan found them?" Callie's eyes are huge against the pale moonlight and she keeps redirecting her focus from my face to my wrist that's wrapped in gauze.

I want to touch her, but I'm afraid to. "I mean, he got a hold of them." I shrug then shrug again, my shoulders feeling as heavy as pounds of rocks. "They're at a hospital. They've been in there for a while. I guess there was some kind of accident and my father's hurt pretty bad or something."

Her eyes enlarge even more. "What exactly is wrong with him?"

"I'm not sure." I scratch at my wrist, making the fresh cut burn. The sensation is both soothing and frightening, a love/hate thing. "Dylan didn't know all the details yet, probably because my mother wouldn't give them to him, but I guess he's been in the hospital for a few weeks now.

Not sure why yet—what's exactly wrong with him."

Callie places her hand over mine, probably so I'll stop scratching at my wrist. "How do you not know all this, though?" she asks. "I mean, how did your brother get a hold of them?"

I swallow the lump in my throat caused by her fingers so close to the cut, a cut we both know came from my own hand. "Tyler broke down and spilled it to Dylan. I guess he'd been with them for a while, but after the accident with my father, he took off and started hitchhiking to Dylan's house."

"And where are your mother and father now? I mean, I know they're in a hospital, but where exactly?"

"I'm not sure. Dylan said all Tyler gave was a phone number. He said he's still trying to get all the details from my mother, but it's like pulling teeth." I smash my lips together so tightly they go numb. "That's how my family is, Callie. They keep secrets—from each other, from the world. No one knows who the Owens are, not even the Owens." I'm about to start crying again, which is fucking ridiculous. I don't need to be crying over anything. Honestly, I don't know what to feel. All those years of being beaten, both mentally and physically, are rendering me useless at feeling the right things in this type of situation.

"I think I'm broken," I whisper as a tear or two falls

from my eyes. I feel like such a fucking pussy. This is ridiculous. Crying over something so stupid. Something I shouldn't be crying over.

Shaking her head, Callie climbs over the console and situates herself on my lap, facing me with a leg on each side. "You're not broken, Kayden. Why would you ever say that?"

"Because..." My hands start to quiver as she guides my arms around her waist. "Because a tiny part of me doesn't even feel bad for him." Before I can see her reaction, which I'm sure is filled with disgust, I lower my head onto her shoulder and breathe in her comforting scent.

After a few minutes of gripping onto her and sobbing, I manage to get my crying under control, but the silence in the car is heavier than my tears. I'm not sure what to say to her, what she's thinking, feeling. God, I wish I could read her mind, see into her soul like I swear she sees into mine.

"You know that day when you beat up Caleb?" she finally asks, her voice slightly choked up.

It's not what I was expecting her to say, but I still lean back to look at her as I nod. "Of course I remember it. It was the day I felt like I finally did something for you instead of the other way around."

I'd lost it that day when I found out Caleb Miller, a

guy who was a little bit older than me and had grown up in our town. I'd wanted him to pay for raping Callie, so I did the only thing I could think of—I beat the shit out of him.

"Well, I remember when I heard about it—about what you did to Caleb." Her voice cracks. "I hated to admit it, considering all of the bad stuff that happened afterward to you, but a part of me felt relieved, maybe even a little bit grateful."

"But you deserved to feel that way," I assure her. "What he did to you was fucking horrible and sick and wrong."

"And so was what you father did to you," she says with pressing eyes. When I start to look away, she places her hand on the side of my face and forces me to look at her. "Kayden, I've heard some of the stories about the things he's done, and I'm pretty sure you've made sure not to tell me the worst of them, considering"—she glances down at my chest—"how big some of those scars are."

"But I don't want to be like him," I say in a strangled whisper. "I don't want to be full of rage and hate like him."

"Why would you ever think you're like him? You're not in any way, shape, or form."

"But I'm relieved because he's hurt, like he deserved it somehow. And that's something he would do—feel relief by hurting people."

"That's different, Kayden. Way, way different. And you didn't hurt him."

She's pretty much saying what my therapist said to me today when I went to talk to him about how I was feeling. Part of me gets why they're telling me this, but the other part of me—the one that fears turning out like my grandfather and my father—can't get over how packed with hate my reaction is.

"I know, but..." I can't meet her gaze, my eyes on the parking lot, the stars in the sky, anywhere other than on her.

"But what?" She urges me to tell her, to look at her, to not shut down like I have in the past. And I want to give her that. I really do, but I need to figure out how.

"What if I keep getting set off?" I finally dare say, forcing my attention back on her.

Her gaze swallows me up. "I'm not sure what you mean."

I raise my wrist. "What if things only get worse and return to this. The last time my father was in my life, this shit owned me."

Worry masks her face. "But he's not in your life anymore."

"He might be. I mean, what if the rest of my family takes him back? And Dylan... he wants me to come out there for a week. I think he suggested it because he thought it'd help being around him while going through this, but I don't know." I shrug. "I've never associated my family with helping me in any way. Even Dylan."

"Then don't go," she states simply, cupping my face between her hands, making me look at her. "You're not under any obligation to go there. You've suffered enough, and if you think this is going to be hard, then you deserve not to go. You have me, Seth, and Luke all here for you, so you're not alone in any of this. You're never, *ever* alone."

I'm starting to get choked up again, but for different reasons. "I know that, but I feel guilty that you guys have to put up with my shit. And I feel guilty for bailing on my family."

"Well, you don't need to feel guilty about anything." Her voice shakes with anger, startling me. "You don't owe them anything, only yourself, so do what *you* want to do and no one else."

"But what if… what if *she* calls me?"

"You mean your mom?"

"Yeah, I'm not sure I ever want to talk to her again." I hate that I sound like a scared, little boy, but I can't seem to control it. My mother was the type of woman who pretended not to see anything, even though she saw *everything*. All those years, she let my father beat me, even called me in sick for school when I was too broken to attend. "Sometimes, I feel like I hate her just as much as my father." I raise my hands between us and let my head fall into them. "God, I don't want to do this—go back to that shit. I thought I'd moved on from it."

"You don't have to let her into your life. If they don't make you happy, don't let them in. Life is all about the happiness, Kayden, and you should never settle for anything less." Callie opens the driver side door so she can climb out of the car. "Now scoot over. I'm going to take you somewhere."

I lift my head up to look at her. "But what about the concert? You were looking forward to this... I can go back inside. It's probably better if I do, anyway, instead of sitting out here, having a pity party."

She rolls her eyes, lightening the mood a smidgeon. "You're not having a pity party." She folds her arms around herself, shivering as her breath puffs out. "And besides, it wasn't the concert I was looking forward to so much as spending time with you all dressed up."

"And I want to give that to you. You deserve to have what you want."

Her intense gaze is locked on mine. "I have what I want every single day."

Is it possible to fall in love with someone even when you're already in love with them? Because I'm pretty sure I just did.

"Where are we going?"

She motions for me to scoot over to the passenger seat. "No way. I'm not telling. You're just going to have to trust me."

It only takes me a beat to move over because, in the end, I do trust her more than anyone else in my life.

Chapter 10

#146 Relive the Best Part of the Past.

Callie

He freaked me out. Not with what he said about his feelings toward his family—that's understandable—but he cut himself again and has that lost look in his eyes like he did last year when he was pushing me away. And while it's not as bad as it was, it still has me worried I might lose him to himself if he decides to enfold back into that dark place inside his head.

Yes, I know I probably could live without him if I had to, know life would have to go on, but God dammit, I don't want to live my life without Kayden. He means more to me than anyone else that has ever been in my life. Whether he realizes it or not, he saved me once when I was stuck in my own dark place. And I want to show him so he'll under-stand how much he means to me, that he is important, that he's a good person, and that happiness does exist every single day when he's with me.

The first place I take him to is the campus. I know he's

completely confused when I pull into the mostly vacant parking lot and park the car as close as I can to the main entrance.

"You know it's almost midnight," Kayden says, unbuckling his seatbelt. "If someone sees us, they might call the cops, especially considering it's Halloween."

"I know." I unfasten my own seatbelt, open the door, and the night breeze gusts into the car. "But it's worth the risk. I promise."

Confused, he gets out of the car and meets me at the front, slipping his fingers through mine. We walk silently across the icy grass, holding hands, and counting the stars. In the distance, I can hear the sounds of shouting and music, probably from a party, but still, the emptiness around us makes me feel at peace.

"This alone is making me feel better." Kayden shucks off his jacket. "Other than you look like you're freezing to death."

"I'm fine," I assure him, but he makes me take his jacket anyway. I slip my arms through the sleeves and breathe the musky scent of his cologne.

"Smell good?" He cracks a smile for the first time tonight when he notices me sniffing his jacket.

"I like the smell of you," I admit, taking another deep inhale. His smile expands and makes my heart do the same

97

thing. "I'm glad you're smiling; I was getting worried."

He sighs, the smile vanishing from his face. "I hate that I make you worry so much."

"You worry about me all the time," I point out, "and whether or not I'm getting what I deserve, which I am."

His lips part to argue, but then he seals them back up when I come to a stop in the center of the sidewalk. The only thing nearby is the historical looking main office of the university and a few trees and benches.

"So this"—I gesture at the ground with my hand—"is the first thing I want to show you."

His brows furrow as he stares down at the concrete. "Okay... It's a really nice spot of sidewalk, I guess." He elevates his gaze back up at me. "I'm so confused."

"I can tell." I'm fighting not to laugh at him, but his puzzlement is cute. "This is where you first ran into me. Literally."

Recognition clicks. "Shit, I remember that. I was trying to catch a football Luke threw and totally took you out." He shakes his head, but the rigidness in his body is starting to unravel. "I can't believe you ever went out with me after that."

"I didn't want to," I admit. "Or I was afraid of you anyway."

"I don't blame you. I'm surprised you didn't get hurt."

"No, I wasn't afraid of you because of that."

"What do you mean?" he wonders, getting confused all over again. "Why were you afraid of me then?"

I tug on his arm, pulling him in the direction of the car. "Come on and I'll show you."

"Okay, I know this restaurant," he says proudly after the waitress seats us in a corner booth that's decorated with a glowing pumpkin and a purple and black lantern. It's late enough that there's hardly anyone here except for a few drunk college kids in the bar area dressed up for Halloween. "This is where we first had dinner. But it wasn't a date. Luke and Seth were here."

"I remember." I'm all smiles as I open my menu. "But it was the closest thing I had ever had to a date."

"Callie, I'm sorry"—he frowns—"that you were so alone for so long."

"I didn't bring you here to feel sorry for me, Kayden." I glance up from the menu and meet his gaze. "My being alone was based on the fact that I didn't trust anyone. But that night, I trusted you."

"Really?" he asks doubtfully as he flips open the menu in front of him. "You seemed like you didn't want to have anything to do with me, especially when I reached out to take your hand."

"That's because I was terrified. I had to run to the bathroom to empty out my stomach," I explain. When he starts to say something, I add, "I didn't bring you here to talk about my past problems. I've done enough of that to last me a lifetime." I reach across the table and place my hand over his. "I brought you here to show you this." I nod at my hand on his. "This is possible because of you."

He shakes his head. "No, this is possible because you're strong. You're the strongest person I've ever met, Callie. I swear to God, I don't know how you do it."

"I do it because I have good people in my life that make everything worth it."

He sighs, disheartened. "You're always glowing with positivity. I wish I could be like that."

"Yeah, *now* I am. But if you would have talked to me before college, you wouldn't have thought so. I was weak back then."

His hand begins to tremble beneath mine. "That's not true. Remember that night... that night you stepped in when,"—he lowers his voice—"when my father was beating me. It takes a shitload of strength to do that."

"And it takes a shitload of strength to survive that," I

press, giving his hand a gentle squeeze. "And to tell someone about it. Like you did."

He grits his teeth. "Eventually, but I put you through
hell until I did."

"It took me forever with Caleb." My pressing tone
meets his. "It took me almost seven years to tell anyone...
and you didn't put me through hell."

He doesn't know what to say. Kayden has always been
great at trying to give me confidence, but being on the re-
ceiving end of the line has always been a struggle for him.
In high school, I would have never guessed it. Being the
gorgeous, star quarterback, dating the most popular girl in
school, I'd thought he radiated self-worth. Boy, was I
wrong.

"I wish things could have been different for you," he
utters softly, tracing my knuckles with his thumb. "I wish
you could have been happy all of your life."

"Yeah, it would have been nice," I agree. "I know it
might sound crazy—and trust me, I wish more than anything I never knew Caleb—but the thing is, what happened
to me did happen. I can't change it, so there's no use letting
it ruin my life. I don't need to give Caleb that kind of power over me anymore. And besides, I might not be here with
you if my life went another path, so I can look at the bad as
something I had to go through to get to the good. You are

my good, no matter what you want to believe. I'm sitting here, happier than I've ever been, because of you. *You* are my happiness."

His gaze is flickering from my eyes to my mouth... from my eyes to my mouth... eyes... mouth. "Can I kiss you right now?" he whispers when he's solely fixated on my lips. "I really need to kiss you."

I nod eagerly. "Yes, please."

As he leans over the table, I meet him halfway, smashing my lips to his and willingly sinking into a passionate kiss right there in public. We don't come up for air until the waitress interrupts us to take our orders. Once she's gone, Kayden stares at me from across the table with a contemplative expression.

"What?" I touch my cheek self-consciously. "Do I have something on my face? I am, after all, wearing enough lipstick to paint a clown's face."

He shakes his head. "It's nothing." He extends his hand toward me and rests his hand on the side of my face. "Listening to you talk—the things you say, the way you look at life—you always make me feel better when I'm down. You're amazing."

"So are you." I relax into his touch. "We make the perfect couple."

When he swallows hard, I think he's going to go back to his self-doubt about his worth so he shocks me when he says, "I think I want to... I want to live with you... You and me together." He pauses then shakes his head determinedly. "No. Scratch that. I *know* I want to."

My heart pitter-patters inside my chest. I don't want to get too excited, but I am. "Are you sure? Because I don't want you to feel pressured or anything. I can wait."

The corners of his mouth tip upward, his expression full of warmth. "I've never been more positive about anything in my life than I am about you. I don't want to ever lose you... I just want to make sure you're happy."

"I am happy. I promise."

"And I want to move in with you. *I promise.*"

Unable to control my excitement any longer, I grin like a big goof. He grins back at me, a genuine smile too. We remain that way, smiling like two silly, love-struck college kids until the waitress strolls up with our drinks and food and gives us a questioning look, probably thinking our goofy, elated expressions are because we're high.

After she sets our plates and drinks down in front of us, Kayden scoops up his burger and takes a large bite. "So, is this our last stop for the night? Or is there more?"

I pick up a handful of fries. "What do you think?"

"I think considering the path you're following, there's

still more." He opens his mouth and takes another massive bite of his burger, appearing so much more relaxed than he did twenty minutes ago. It makes me want to keep going down this path.

"So, if you had to guess the next place, where do you think it would be?" I pluck the onion off my burger as I wait for his answer, wondering if he's cracked the code of my path.

"You think I don't know," he says amusedly, "but I do."

I shrug, equally amused. "I'm curious if you remember."

His brow arches. "And what do I win if I get it right?"

"Whatever you want," I tease then bit down of my burger.

He seems pleased, a big grin plastered on his face. "Prepare to lose then." He reaches across the table to wipe some mayo off my lip. "Races, spray paint, and green footprints."

He doesn't have to say exactly where it is—we both know what those words mean. Such a simple night, at least to an outsider's point of view, but to me, it was one of the most magical, life-changing nights of my life.

Chapter 11
#149 Channel Your Inner Daredevil.

Callie

Thirty minutes later, we're entering the store we'd gone to that night over a year ago, the one Kayden, Seth, Luke and I stopped at right before we went and tagged a rock at a very famous tagging area. I was a little buzzed that night and felt so free hanging out with the three of them because it was the first time I had felt like I had friends.

The store is still the same, a little rundown and selling cheap stuff for cheap prices. Kayden and I instantly make our way to the aisle where, that night, I had stepped on a can of green spray paint and gotten it all over the floor. It was during a sort of wrestling match between Kayden and me after Luke had turned the night into a game.

"Holy shit. I can't believe you can still see it?" Kayden says as we both stare at the faint green shoe print still staining the dingy linoleum floor.

I slap my hand over my mouth as a giggle escapes. "I

should feel bad, right?"

Kayden shakes his head as I move my foot over the print—the perfect fit. "No way. If anything, you should feel proud. You marked that night forever."

"Well, as long as this store exists, but it was definitely a night to be marked." I pause and then decide to admit the truth. "You know, when we were in the cab by ourselves, I kind of wanted you to kiss me. Although, I probably would have freaked out if you did, so maybe it's a good thing you didn't. I don't think I was quite ready for it yet."

As he processes my words, he steps toward me, our bodies just inches away from one another. "I wanted to kiss you that night, but I was afraid."

I inch toward him, stealing what little space is remaining between us. "Of what?"

"That I would like it. That it would be wrong because I had a girlfriend. That I wasn't good enough for you." He wets his lips with his tongue, his attention fixed on my lips. "Should we have a do-over?"

I nod enthusiastically, and without any hesitation, his mouth collides with mine so forcefully I wonder if the impact will leave a bruise. But I don't care. Let me bruise. All I can concentrate on is his tongue parting my lips as he consumes me. The force sends me backward, and I slam into the shelf behind me, another bruise perhaps, but again, it doesn't matter. I don't plan on breaking this kiss for anything.

But the shelf is lined with cans of spray paint and when we ram into it, a row of them tip over and fall onto the floor, making a lot of noise.

I sputter a laugh as we break the kiss and stare down at the mess we just made. "Holy crap," I say. "We're cursed."

"No way," he breathes, his palms splayed on my back beneath my shirt. "It's destiny, letting us have a second chance at the night I should have kissed you."

His words sweep me away from reality, and I grab the front of his shirt to pull him in for another kiss. Right as our lips reunite, someone yells, "What the hell is going on back here?"

Our heads snap in the direction the voice came from. Standing at the end of the aisle is the clerk, red faced and angry as he stares down at the mess we just made. He's about thirty or so, with shoulder length hair, and wearing a name tag on his tie dye shirt that says *Ed*.

"We'll clean it up," I say, but Ed comes storming toward us.

"I'm so sick of you little shits coming in here and thinking it's funny to trash my store." As Ed strides toward us, he presses his finger to his chest as he repeats, "*My*

107

store. Not yours. Mine. I'm going to make you pay for every damn one of those spray paint cans."

I'm not sure what to do. The guy has this creepy look on his face like he's out of his mind and it's frightening but funny at the same time. A nervous laugh leaves my lips as Kayden grabs my hand and tugs me with him as he takes off in the other direction.

The clerk shouts at us to, "Get your punk asses back here now!" but that only makes us move faster and laugh harder.

We don't stop laughing until we're safely in the car and driving down the road toward the mountains, the headlights of Kayden's car lighting the way. I'm still the driver, despite Kayden's protests, because I want to be the one taking him on this journey.

"So where are you taking me now?" Kayden asks as we head up toward the foothills.

"You don't know?" I ask, wondering if he's serious. Considering the direction we're going in, it has to be obvious. Besides, we've had a few good moments up at this place, which makes it a super important part of our past.

He glances at me with a devious look on his face as he lifts his hand. "Actually, I do." In his hand is a can of spray paint, which means he knew where we were going before we even got in the car. I'd be happy about this, and I am, except... "Did you shoplift that can of paint?"

"The guy was a stoned asshole; I couldn't very well pay for it with him trying to attack us," he says, and when I sigh, he laughs. "Relax, Callie. I threw a few bucks down on the floor before we left." He draws a line down my cheekbone with his fingertip, eliciting an eye flutter from me. "I know you're too nice to condone shoplifting."

"Hey, I can be a rebel," I say, half joking, half serious. "I've drank while underage."

He chuckles at my lame statement. "You're so adorable."

Gripping onto the wheel with one hand, I aim a finger at him. "Hey, mister, I am not always adorable. And I'm going to prove it to you." *I am?*

That gets him to smile, which makes me smile, too, even though I have no clue how to back up my words. Still, I rack my brain for a way to show him the daredevil side of me that I'm not sure I've discovered yet.

The idea comes to me when I pull up to the parking spot at the bottom of the hill. I remember how Seth is always making jokes about how people come up here and have sex. I blushed like crazy when he told me that Greyson and him came up here once.

I'm not even sure I can go through with it. Yeah, I'm a

different person than I used to be. Much stronger and I blush less. Plus, there's no one else up here tonight so we have the whole place to ourselves.

"What's going on in that beautiful head of yours?" Kayden asks, interrupting my dazedness.

I tear my attention from the trees in front of the car and rotate in my seat to face him. The headlights are still on, and between that and the moonlight, I can make out his firm jawline, soft lips, and wonderfully familiar eyes.

"Callie." He starts to squirm under the weight of my gaze. "What's going on? Is something wrong?"

Shaking my head, I swallow my nerves and click the headlights off. We're smothered by darkness, which makes it easier to do what I'm about to. Or maybe it's the costume making me feel like someone else, someone who can take risks, be a daredevil. I really don't care where the feeling's coming from. I just do what Seth's always saying and roll with it, leaning over the console and kissing Kayden without any warning. He sucks in a sharp breath as my lips brush his and then he laughs softly when my tongue sweeps across his lip, signaling that I want him to open up.

"I feel like you're about ready to show me just how un-adorable you are," he murmurs in this low, husky voice that sends a thrill through me.

"You're completely right," I tell him as I tug off my boots then climb over the console and onto his lap. I put a knee on each side of him then crash my lips against his. This time, he opens right up, sucking my tongue into his mouth and kissing me back with equal intensity. He nips at my bottom lip as he wraps his fingers around the back of my head and guides me closer, until there's no room left between our bodies.

We've started to fog up the windows as I begin to unbutton his shirt, but he catches my hand in his. "Callie, wait. We don't have to do this," he pants against my lips, sounding as if stopping is the last thing he wants to do. "I didn't mean to upset you with the adorable comment."

"You didn't upset me. I promise." And it's the truth. Right now, my mind is moving a million miles an hour, my body running on some sort of adrenaline high, and I want to keep going, keep doing new things with Kayden, make every moment count, just like I'm always saying.

Before he can work up another protest, I slip my hand from his hold and flick another button loose on his shirt. I continue my way down it until I've got them all undone, then he slips the plaid shirt off and chucks it in the backseat. I'm about to reach for the hem of his T-shirt to take that off too, when he leans toward the passenger side and turns the key so the battery clicks on and heat blasts

111

from the vents.

"Trust me. You don't want it being freezing in here. It might do weird things to my man parts," he jokes and then peels his T-shirt off while I giggle at his comment. He's laughing as he reaches for the zipper of the jacket I have on and then yanks it down. After he gets it off, he tugs the straps of my dress down enough that my bra is exposed. Then he jerks down the front of it so my breasts hit the air.

Before I can even react to the still somewhat chilly air, his mouth is on me, sucking and nipping and driving my body mad. It's amazing how, even after a year, he still makes me feel the same overwhelming excitement and vulnerability I felt the first time we were together. It never gets old, whether we're in his bed or in the crammed seat of a car.

My head falls back as he continues to devour me with his mouth, moving back and forth between my breasts, only stopping when I'm on the verge of passing out from lack of oxygen. Then he undoes the button of his jeans, and before I can even ask what he's doing, he reaches up the bottom of my dress to slip my panties off. I decide to help him out and lift my hips up, snorting a laugh when I bump my head on the roof. However, all humor fades when he pulls me back down to his lap and thrusts himself inside me.

It's either the angle of my hips or the way my legs are bent, but he sinks in deep, and I swear to God every one of my nerve endings explode as I gasp, clutching onto the back of the seat. It's intense. No, beyond intense, to the point where I don't think I can breathe.

"Jesus," Kayden utters in a hoarse whisper as he grips at my waist from underneath my dress. "This feels…"

"Amazing," I finish for him then start rocking my hips, unable to hold still a second longer.

We move rhythmically, completely in sync with each other, like we were made for each other, which in my opinion, we are. There's no one else in the world that will make me feel the way Kayden does. I will never trust anyone more. Never want to be with anyone as much. He's it for me, and I only hope that it's the same way for him. That he wants to move in with me like he's said. Be with me.

Maybe forever.

Chapter 12

#150 Rewrite Beautiful Words in Your Own Beautiful Way.

Kayden

"That was..." I can barely breathe, let alone finish the sentence. Not after that. Sex in a car with Callie. How the hell did a really shitty night turn into something so amazing? I'd been so upset about all the stuff with my dad and how it was making me feel so ugly inside. Plus, I'd had a relapse. I felt like I was sinking toward the bottom of despair, and now, I feel like I'm on cloud nine, running on fucking rainbows. But I don't think it's just the sex but the memories that are doing it to me too. Through all of the craziness and crappiness that's occurred, I'd somehow lost sight of all the good stuff that has happened and is still happening.

"I must be good if I'm making you speechless." Callie tries to be playful, but even through the dark, I can tell she's blushing by the way she turns her head and lets strands of hair fall into her face.

114

"You're perfect." I taste her lips one more time before I help her put her bra back into place then the straps of her dress. She shivers as my fingers brush her shoulders, and it makes me smile that my touch still does this to her after almost a year. "You always are."

She smiles as she hops back into the driver's seat so I can put my shirt back on. "I feel like I'm high," she admits as she slips her panties back on.

"So you like being naughty?" I tease as I button up my plaid shirt.

Slipping her foot into her boot, she shrugs, but her lips threaten to turn upward. "Maybe."

I want to tell her she's adorable, but that's kind of what started this whole thing to begin with. Okay, maybe I should call her it again. Hell, I need to start calling her it a lot more.

Before I can say anything else, though, she pushes open the door to get out. "Are you ready to visit the next place?" she asks, wiggling her other foot into her boot before she swings her feet out onto the ground.

I nod, grabbing the can of spray paint from the center console before I hop out of the car with her. She slips on her jacket and then I take her hand as soon as we reach the path, unable to keep myself from touching her. That's the thing with Callie—something as simple as her touch can warm the cold inside me. And her words are even more powerful. They not only warm the cold, but melt it into a puddle.

It's what her words did for me at the restaurant. It's why I told her I want to move in with her. I think I always have wanted to do it. I simply wasn't able to say it until that moment when I realized, not only how much she means to me, but how much I mean to her. I may fight it, may worry I'm not good enough for her, but in the end, I'm what she seems to want, and she deserves to have what she wants. Therefore, I'm giving it to her—giving myself to her.

"We probably should have brought flashlights," Callie remarks as the path starts to wind into the hills, making the city lights below disappear and our surroundings shadow over.

I reach into my pocket to get my phone and swipe my finger across the screen so it lights up. "How about this?" I hold it up and aim it down on the path.

"You're brilliant," she says then picks up the pace, pretty much skipping through the dark.

"Careful." I grip onto her hand as she starts to slip on a patch of ice.

As she keeps skipping, I end up shuffling after her until we reach the steep rock I once sat on with her before we'd even kissed. There's a light layer of snow on some of the rocks and icy spots on the ground.

"I'm not sure we should climb up that in the dark," I tell her, pulling her back toward me until her back is pressed against my chest.

"But we climbed them in the dark before," she says as I circle my arms around my waist.

"I know, but I love you now and would die if anything happened to you." I kiss the sensitive spot behind her ear and she sighs.

"All right, you win, but only because you made such a beautiful argument." She takes a seat on a small rock on the ground and faces the path we just walked up. "Remember how each time we came up here, you had to help me climb up the rocks?"

I nod and sit on the rock beside her, turning the timer on my screen so it's at the max—we have ten minutes of light. "I also remember how I had a naughty dream about you where I was helping you down the rocks." I set the phone down beside my feet and try to get comfortable even though the ground is freezing my ass.

Her head snaps in my direction. "What? When?"

"The night after we first came here."

"But you were still dating Daisy then."

"It didn't mean I wasn't attracted to you," I tell her.

"Trust me, I was. Way, way attracted to you."

She presses her lips together as if she wants to say something but is fighting it.

"What's on your mind?" I brush my finger across the inside of her wrist.

Her shoulders rise and fall as she heavy-heartedly shrugs. "You know, I never got how you were attracted to me when you were dating Daisy. I mean, I know you love me now, but it never made sense why you'd break up with her, then want to date me right after. I mean, I know she was a bitch, but she was... Well, she was really, really pretty." A thousand protests run through my mind, but before I can say anything, she adds, "I'm not saying that so you'll compliment me. I know you love me. I was just telling you how I felt in the past since this is a night about the past."

It takes me a moment to find my voice, but only because I'm still shocked about what she said.

"First of all, let's get something straight," I tell her. "All looks aside, you are a thousand times a better person than Daisy will ever be. The girl was more than a bitch. She was evil and self-centered. She never asked about my scars, never tried to get to know me in the way you did, where I felt completely and utterly vulnerable but in a way I needed to be. You saved me, Callie, not only from my father, but from myself and a life full of misery and self-loathing. And yeah, I know I still have a ways to go, but you still help me, even now."

"Good, I'm glad. I love helping—"

I cover her mouth with my hand, silencing her. "I'm not done yet." I position my hands so her face is trapped between them, wishing it wasn't so dark so I could see my favorite part about her—her eyes. "And second of all, you're a million times more beautiful than Daisy ever will be." She starts to immediately protest, but I talk over her. "And not just because you're beautiful on the inside, which I know you're about ready to say, but because you are ridiculously beautiful in a way that almost seems unreal sometimes."

"Kayden, I appreciate you saying that, but I know I'm not," she says. "I know what I am, which is average, and I'm okay with that."

"You'll never be average, Callie." I wish she'd get the full extent of what I'm trying to say. "Daisy was like plastic—all fake nails and tanner, bleached hair, and fancy clothes—nothing about her was real. *You*"—I bring her lips closer to me—"you're real. Everything from your freckles to those beautiful, gorgeous eyes of yours, to those fucking perfect lips. You're unconventionally beautiful, the kind of beautiful people can't even understand because it's not generic and created—it just is."

She's quiet for what feels like an eternity, the soft sound of her breathing filling the silence between us. "You're turning into quite the master of words," she says softly. "You just put this writer to shame."

My lips tug upward, but I'm not ready to smile just yet. "But you get what I'm saying, right? You understand how beautiful you are inside and out?"

When she nods, I feel her cheeks move as she smiles. "But only if you understand just how much I need you and how much I deserve you."

It takes a lot for me to say it, but I know I have to— know it's right for the moment. "All right, it's a deal," I say then lean in to kiss her, taking my time, savoring the feel of her lips.

I pull away about eight minutes later when the screen clicks off and darkness surrounds us. Picking it up, I reset it for another ten minutes then take the spray can out of my pocket. "So, what are you planning on putting on the rock this time?" I ask, giving the can to her.

"Hmmm…." She taps her finger against her lip then hands the can back to me. "I think you should be the one to do it this time."

"No way. You're the writer."

She gets to her feet and brushes the dirt and snow off her ass. "Nope. I'm giving you the honors tonight since you've been on a roll with beautiful words." When I don't get up right away, she offers her hand to me. "Come on, Kayden. After what you just said to me, this should be a piece of cake."

I thread my fingers through hers and get to my feet, giving the can a little shake. Then I stare at the rock. And stare at the rock.

And stare.

And stare.

And stare.

"It's like when I look at my computer screen sometimes." She playfully pokes me in the side. "Only, instead of a cursor doing the tormenting, it's a can of paint."

I lift the can to write something, but the pressure is getting to me. My mind is blank until I suddenly get an idea as I remember the first night we came up here. Callie had painted her own quote on the wall... that amazing quote.

Smiling, I press the nozzle and move my hand across the rock. She grabs the phone and aims it so I can see better and so she can read what I'm writing. When I'm done, I stand back beside her and she reads it aloud.

"*In the existence of our lives, there are many coincidences that bring people together, but there's only one person that will own your heart forever,*" she reads aloud, and I swear she almost cries near the end.

"Someone really smart once wrote that, I think," I say as I put the lid back on.

"She didn't say that exactly." She turns to face me. "And I like your version a lot better."

"Good." I take her hand and hold onto to it for a thousand different reasons—to touch her, to feel comforted, to keep on standing, living, breathing. It's crazy how the night went from shitty to one of the best nights I've had in a long time. It makes me realize how much I need her and how much I need to keep working on being the guy she deserves. "Because I mean it—all of it.

Chapter 13

#153 Help Someone Even When They Don't Necessarily Ask For Help.

Callie

The next few weeks go by in a blur of fall leaves, midterms, and football games. Before I know it, Thanksgiving is approaching. Kayden and I haven't gotten a place of our own yet, nor have we really talked about it since that night. But he does seem to be doing a lot better after we spent time reliving some of our past moments, and that's really all that matters, right?

I also haven't noticed any fresh cuts on his skin, and he hasn't gotten upset over anything with his family, so things are going pretty smoothly. Then again, I don't think much has happened other than Dylan calling to check in and to see if Kayden is planning on going out there for Thanksgiving break.

"So have you decided what you're going to do yet?" I ask Kayden. He stopped by my dorm after football practice while I was in the middle of folding my laundry. There are piles of clothes on the bed, and I'm still working on the pile in the basket. By the time I get finished, there will probably be more to clean and fold.

Kayden is lying on the floor since there's no room anywhere else, throwing a football up in the air and catching it. "About Thanksgiving?"

I nod, folding a shirt and adding it to a stack near the foot of the bed. "I was just wondering if you decided whether you're going to go to Virginia or not." It's a sensitive subject so I keep my voice light.

He tosses the football in the air and catches it before he responds. "What do you think I should do?" he asks, tipping his head back to look at me.

I grab a pair of jeans from the basket. "Kayden, I don't really think I should make that choice for you."

"Yeah, I guess I worded that wrong." He sets the football down and rolls to his side so he can easily look at me. "I just meant... I mean, what are you doing?"

"For Thanksgiving?" I shrug as I fold the jeans. "Going home. You know how my mom is with holidays. She'd be super upset if I didn't come home. You can come with me, though, if you don't want to go to Virginia."

He bobs his head up and down, contemplating something. "Yeah, I don't think I'm up for going back home really." He seems guilty about it, which he shouldn't be.

"You don't have to think of it as going home. Just visiting my family for Thanksgiving."

"Yeah, but not thinking of it as home is part of the problem because it never really was for me." He flips on his stomach and pushes himself up to his feet, his grey T-shirt riding up just enough for me to get a little glimpse of his firm stomach. "And I think I want to find some sort of place that I can call home." He wavers. "So I think maybe I should go to Virginia and try out this whole holiday thing with Dylan. I mean, he hasn't brought up anything about my mom or dad lately, so I should be okay... I think... maybe it's a good idea. And besides, I think it's time I tried to handle that stuff"—he glances at the healing scar on his wrist—"so I don't slip up again."

I feel a pang of sadness in my stomach at the idea of spending a week away from him. Plus, there'd almost be a country's worth of distance between us. Yet I know those are both selfish reasons, and in the end, it would be really nice for him to be able to get along with Dylan, especially if he wants to.

"If you feel like you should go to Virginia, then you should go to Virginia." I collect a stack of jeans to put in the dresser. "It'd be good for you to get to know Dylan and maybe even Tyler if he's going to be there and you think you want to see him."

"I think he'll be in rehab, from what Dylan told me." He scoops up the football from the floor as I open the drawer and put the clothes in. "But I might get to see him for a little bit. I think, anyway."

"Good." Mustering up my best smile, I turn to face him. I'm happy for him and everything, but I just hope everything goes well. I worry. "I'll miss you, though."

"You could always come with me," he says with hope as he clutches onto the football.

"I wish I could, but I already told my mom I'd come home. Plus, Jackson's going to be there, and I haven't seen him since Spring Break. And I made a number on the list to try to have a better relationship with him." I point at my door where the whiteboard with the to-do list usually is, but furrow my brows when I realize it's gone.

"What on earth. Where's my list?" I glance at Kayden. "Was it here when you came over today?"

He shrugs, rotating the football in his hand. "I have no idea."

I scratch my head. "Maybe Seth took it for some reason." I start to reach for my phone. "I should call him and ask."

"But anyway," Kayden says, clearly cutting me off,

"that's good you're trying to patch up things with your brother." He grabs my hand as I give him a questioning look. "I know that's been hard for you, considering Caleb was his best friend."

I decide to ignore his weird sidetracking thing—for now anyway—but I will get to the bottom of what caused it.

"He's been really nice since I finally told him what happened," I say as Kayden gives my arm a tug and lures me toward him. "I don't want to be mad at him anymore. It was too exhausting, and there's no point in holding grudges."

The corner of his lips tip to a half smile. "You always say stuff that I feel pertains to me."

"Oh, that's not what I meant," I begin to protest as our bodies greet each other. "What happened between Jackson and I isn't the same as what your father and mother did to you. At all." I feel horrible for what I've said. Kayden should be able to hold a grudge against his father and mother for forever in my opinion. Stuff like that doesn't just evaporate. The large scar on Kayden's side proves it.

"Callie, relax. I know you weren't referring to me." He gently tugs on a loose strand of my hair. "I was just teasing you."

I assess him carefully. He seems like he's being honest

127

and looks almost happy. "You seem like you're in a good mood. What's up?"

He rolls his tongue in his mouth to keep from smiling. "It's nothing. I'm just happy I'm here with you."

I tip my head and study him suspiciously. "No, something's up. You're like super happy, and you just purposely sidetracked me from the fact that the list is missing from the door."

"Okay, maybe there is something going on." He's so cute, trying to restrain a grin. "But I can't tell you right now."

"Is it bad?"

"No. It's good, I think." He's totally enjoying this.

"Okay, now I really want to know." I pout out my lip. "Please?"

Chuckling under his breath, he reaches up and touches my bottom lip with his fingertip. "That trick's not going to work on me."

"What trick?" I ask innocently.

He gives me a look. "Are you trying to tell me that you don't purposefully pout your lip out when you're attempting to get your way?" he asks, and I get a guilty look on my face. "Yeah, see. I can read you just as well as you can read me." He winks at me then pulls me in for a kiss, dropping the football to the floor. Our tongues instantly tangle, and within seconds, he's picking me up and carrying me toward the bed.

I have every intention of pulling off his clothes and re-experiencing the moment we shared in the car a few weeks ago, but then the door swings open and Harper comes walking in.

"Oh, shit." She halts in the doorway when she spots us on the bed, legs entwined, bodies pressed together, hands all over each other—thankfully, no one's clothes have come off.

"Sorry," I apologize, sitting up while Kayden remains lying down, his fingers sketching up and down my back. "We were just..." How am I supposed to finish that sentence? *We were just about to have hot, sweaty sex?* Yeah, that sentence is not coming out of my mouth.

Harper dithers in the doorway, hugging her books to her chest. "I can come back later."

I shake my head and hop off my bed. "No, it's okay. I needed to run to the store anyway." I reach for my jacket as Kayden begrudgingly gets off the bed and picks up his football.

"Hey, could you by chance pick up a roll of tape for me?" Harper asks as she drops her books onto the bed. "I ran out last night."

I nod. "Sure."

"Thanks." She forces a smile as she starts to unbutton her jacket. "Actually, Callie, before you leave... could I talk to you?" She flicks the last button undone then sets her coat on the bedpost, her eyes flicking to Kayden before they land on me. "Alone maybe?"

"Um, yeah, sure." I turn to Kayden who shoots me a puzzled look. "Can I meet you out in the car?"

He nods warily. "Sure." He softly kisses my forehead then glances at Harper before walking out the door.

Once it clicks shut, I face Harper. "So what's up?"

"It's nothing, really." But her expression suggests otherwise as she sinks down on her bed with her shoulders slumped. "Honestly, I don't know how to bring it up to you without you getting mad."

"I won't get mad." I don't know what else to say since I don't know where she's going with this.

Sighing, she fiddles with a strand of her hair, twisting it around her finger. "The other day, I overheard you and Seth talking about stuff." She's staring at her hair, completely fixated on it. "About something that happened to you."

"I'm not sure what you mean." I sit down on my bed so we're facing each other. "Seth and I have said a lot of things," I tell her and then try to make a joke because she looks so sad. "Particularly Seth. He *loves* to talk."

A tiny smile rises on her lips, but her eyes still seem filled with sadness as she looks up at me. "Well, it was the other day. I think you guys thought I had my headphones on and was listening to music, but I was actually trying to find something to listen to, so I heard a little bit of your conversation... about a guy doing stuff to you." She winces as she says it, and even though I'm used to talking about this aloud, I still wince myself.

"Yeah..." Again, I'm unsure of what to say.

"Sorry," she quickly says. "I'm sure you're wondering why I'm saying this, and the truth is... Well, the truth is, I heard you say something about how you were feeling a lot better and that you have been since you talked to your parents about it. I was kind of wondering"—her gaze drops to the space on the floor between our feet—"how you went about that."

"Telling my parents that I was... raped?" It's still so hard to say aloud, even though I've been openly talking about it for a while.

Again, she winces. "Yeah... that." She looks up at me, and although she doesn't say anything about it, I think I suddenly understand why she's bringing this up. I know that pained expression she's trying to keep trapped inside

131

her because I carried the same one for years.

But I'm not sure if I should ask her yet if she was raped. Stuff like this can be tricky—getting someone to tell the truth can be tricky. I should know since it took me almost seven years of carrying around the heaviness inside me, afraid to let it out because I was afraid of what people would think of me, and honestly, I was afraid of Caleb too.

"You don't have to tell me if you don't want to." Harper's words rush out of her. Right now, she seems like a completely different person, but that's because she's vulnerable and scared and not pretending.

"No, it's okay." I lift my shoulders to build up some confidence. "When it came to telling my parents, I just sort of sat them down and told them. There's really not a right or easy way to do it other than to just do it. I do think that getting to the point where you decide you're going to tell someone is the hardest part though."

"Did you struggle with it?" she asks. "I mean, with getting the courage to tell someone."

I suck in a gradual inhale through my nose to keep the emotions inside me so I won't freak her out. "Yeah, it took me almost seven years."

Her eyes snap wide. "How old were you when it happened?"

"Twelve."

"Jesus, Callie, that's horrible."

"Yeah, it was, but I'm trying to move on." I pause, wondering if it's the right time to ask her something I want to know, but then I realize that there might not be a right time, and I just have to do it. "How old were you?"

She sighs, her shoulders slumping. "Is it that obvious why I'm asking all of this?"

"It might not be for someone else, but you have this look on your face right now that I'm kind of familiar with."

"And what look is that?"

"Fear… pain."

We exchange a look of understanding. I've always known that what happened to me has happened to other people, but I've never really discussed it with anyone who's had to live through the hellish experience.

"I feel those things," she utters quietly, her eyes getting watery. "I hate that I do, though. Everyone thinks I'm so happy because that's what I show them, but I'm not as happy as I seem."

"Everyone thought I was crazy," I tell her. "But I did chop off my hair with a pair of scissors and stopped talking to people."

She offers me a sympathetic look. "Callie, that's so sad."

"And so is pretending to be happy all the time," I say. "Everyone should feel okay enough to be themselves."

She nods, agreeing. "Yeah, but my story's not as sad as yours. I was fourteen."

"That doesn't make it any better." I stand up from the bed and cross the room to sit down beside her, my legs feeling the slightest bit wobbly. "Rape is a horrible thing, no matter what, and you should tell someone about it."

"I'm not sure if I can tell my mom." She frowns, and it makes me wonder if perhaps it was somebody living under the same roof as her.

"How about a brother or sister then?" I suggest.

She shakes her head. "I don't have any."

"How about your dad?"

Her expression hardens as she grinds her teeth and balls her hands into fists. "I'm not telling my step-father."

Okay, I'm pretty sure that's probably who did it to her, but I don't want to push her or make assumptions because I can tell she's on the verge of cracking, and I could be wrong. "What about another relative? Or a therapist?"

She considers what I've said for quite a few minutes. "You've talked to a therapist, right? I mean, I thought I heard Seth and you talking about it at the beginning of the school year."

"Yeah, I used to up until a couple of months ago. I can give you her number. She's really nice and understanding and gets things like this."

"Okay, yeah, can I have her number?"

Nodding, I retrieve my phone from my pocket and text Harper the contact information of my therapist. "You should call her today, too, while you're in this place where you can talk about it."

"But I didn't really talk about it," she says with a discouraged sigh. "Not really."

"That's not true." I tuck my phone away. "What you said today was a huge step."

Her lips turn upward, and it looks as though she might be showing me a glimpse of her real smile. I realize, right there and then, that I've never seen it before.

"Well, I'll call her, but we'll see how it goes when it comes time to go there," she says. "I've tried this before and never gotten the courage to do it. I only dared bring it up to you after I heard you talking to Seth about what happened to you because it made me feel like you'd"—she fidgets with a bracelet she's wearing—"understand, I guess."

"A lot of people will understand." I pause, wondering what else I can do to help her because I want to help people who are struggling like I was once. Just thinking about other people out there that have gone through stuff like me and Harper makes me want to find all of them and tell them it'll be okay. I'm not even sure how to do that, but I need to somehow. "If you want me to, I can go with you to your appointment."

"Really?" She perks up, seeming sincerely grateful.

I nod. "Of course."

She blows out a breath, utterly relieved. "Thanks, Callie. And not just for the offer, but for not getting all weirded out. You're really good at this, you know? Talking and understanding and everything."

Her words warm my heart.

"Thanks. And you're welcome," I tell her and head for the door. "Let me know when you get scheduled, and if you ever need to talk, I'm right across the room."

When she nods, I step into the hallway, shut the door behind me, and lean against it. I feel strangely at peace with myself. I'm not even sure if it's because I was able to talk to someone about what happened to me without going into a panic or if it's because I tried to help someone who didn't flat out ask.

"Is everything okay?" Kayden's voice tugs me out of my thoughts.

I turn my head and find him standing to the side of me

with the football tucked under his arm. "Hey, I thought you went down to the car."

He glances from the door back to me. "Nah, I thought I'd wait for you here. Seemed like you might need me after whatever was happening in there."

I stand upright. "No, I'm fine. She just wanted to talk about stuff."

"What kind of stuff?" he asks as we move toward the elevator, holding hands.

"Stuff she's going through," I say vaguely. "Stuff I'd understand."

Thankfully, I think he gets what I'm implying without me having to say it aloud, since I'm pretty sure Harper wouldn't want me talking to anyone about it.

I push the down button with my thumb then face him while I wait for the doors to open. "So, are you going to tell me now why you look so happy today?"

"Nope." His lips twitch with amusement.

"You are the meanest person ever." I jump into the elevator as the doors swing open, yanking him in with me, and he ends up stumbling over his feet. "But that's okay because I love you."

He laughs as I stand on my tiptoes to kiss him, but he quickly pulls back when his phone starts buzzing from inside the back pocket of his jeans. Usually, he ignores calls and texts when we're in a lip lock, so I'm a little surprised when he moves away to take his phone out.

He muses over something as he reads the message on the screen.

I recline against the wall and casually ask, "Who's that?"

He stares at the screen a second longer before texting something back. "No one."

I'm not sure how to respond to his brush off, so I crack a joke. "Well, clearly it's someone, otherwise your phone wouldn't have gone off."

He presses one last button on the screen then returns his phone to his pocket before looking back at me. "It was just a text from Seth."

"And what'd it say?"

He shrugs, bracing a hand on the wall beside my head. "Nothing important really." He leans in to kiss me, but I place a hand on his solid chest and stop him.

"Your jaw's twitching right now," I remark, somewhat amused, but a little upset.

He gives me a mock offended look, pushing back from the wall to press his hand to his chest. "Are you accusing me of lying?"

I narrow my eyes at him, but it's a playful gesture.

"Yeah, that's exactly what I'm doing." I point a finger at him as we arrive at the bottom floor and the elevator doors glide open. "I know you're keeping something from me, and I'm going to find out."

He's completely entertained now as he follows me out of the elevator and toward the exit doors. "And how do you plan on doing that?" He shoots me a confident grin.

"Wow, aren't we a little bit cocky today?" I retaliate with an arrogant squaring of my shoulders as I reach into my pocket. "But we'll see who's the cocky one after I text Seth."

His amusement suddenly shifts to worry as I whip out my phone. "Seth knows he's not supposed to tell you," he says.

I raise my phone up in front of us and wiggle it around, teasing him. "Seth is terrible at keeping secrets. You and I both know that." I really don't have any intention of texting Seth. I'm simply having fun and hoping he'll just tell me whatever his little secret is.

"Callie, don't," he warns, but he's fighting back a smile.

I let mine slip through, though, full on grinning as I run backwards toward the door. "I'm totally doing it." I laugh then whirl around and burst through the doors. Snow is tumbling from the sky and the wind is howling, yet I continue to sprint down the sidewalk toward the parking lot.

I know he's going to catch me soon, my short legs don't stand a chance against his long, very in-shape ones, but I'm still going to try my hardest because it's fun and I'm enjoying myself. And, really, that's kind of the point of everything, isn't it? To enjoy life and have fun. I spent so much time never smiling, laughing, enjoying anything, and I feel like I missed out on so much. But that doesn't mean I can't make up for it now or for the rest of my life.

"You think you can outrun me!" Kayden calls out, laughing as his heavy footsteps close in behind.

"Of course I can!" Laughter sputters from my lungs as I veer to the right and try to sprint across the snowy lawn, but it's chilly enough that the snow is freezing the moment it touches the ground, making it slippery and complicated to run on. I curse as my feet try to part ways from underneath me and my hands shoot out to my sides in an attempt to keep my balance.

Right as I'm about to fall flat on my ass, a set of strong arms wrap around my waist. A split second later, a warm chest presses against my back as I'm helped to my feet.

"You're really asking for it, aren't you?" Kayden whispers in my ear, dragging his teeth across the sensitive spot of flesh right below it as he helps me stand back upright.

I shiver and not from the cold. "Maybe."

His fingers dig into my flesh right below the hem of my black T-shirt. "I'll take your phone as payment for saving your cute, little ass from falling."

I grip my phone in my hand, my eyelashes fluttering against the thick snowflakes. "No way."

He chuckles lowly, a deep noise that vibrates from his chest, and I have to bite down on my lip to keep from whimpering. "Okay, I guess we'll have to do this the hard way."

"Isn't this the hard way, already?" I sound breathless.

He laughs again and then, without warning, his fingers sneak up my shirt, and he starts to tickle me.

"Stop!" I shout through my laughter, my legs giving out on me. I almost buckle to the ground, but he's there to hold me up and keeps tickling me until I almost pee my pants.

"Fine! I surrender! I surrender!" I gasp through my laughter when I'm about one second away from having an accident.

His fingers instantly stop moving, and he kisses the back of my head as he takes the phone from my hand then frees me from his arms.

I spin around and cross my arms over my chest. "That

was cheating."

He grins proudly as he hides my phone in the pocket of his coat. "No way. That was completely fair. It's not my fault you're tiny and adorable." He pokes me in the ribs.

I glare at him, pretending I'm upset. "If it wasn't for the snow, I would have been able to run faster."

"Yeah, but I wasn't really running. Just walking swiftly." He's so smug right now. I've never seen him act like this—so confident. It's sexy, and I can't help but jump onto him and kiss him right there in the middle of a blizzard.

He doesn't hesitate, kissing me back with equivalent hunger, his hands sliding underneath me and cupping my butt. He groans when I bite at his bottom lip, and I gasp as his mouth trails down my jawline, leaving a path of heat simmering against my snow-kissed skin. The mix of heat and ice sends a combustion of sensations swirling throughout my body. It's blissfully amazing. Mind-blowing. I want more.

"We should go back to your dorm," I say, my head tipping back as his mouth finds the hollow of my neck. I tangle my fingers through his wet hair and guide him closer. "Or someplace where we can be alone…" I trail off as his phone starts going off in his pocket, and this time, I'm not as surprised when he breaks the kiss, but I'm equally as disappointed.

I sigh, hopping off him as he retrieves his phone. He reads the screen and then grins. "You know what? That sounds like a great idea," he says, lacing our fingers together as he tugs me toward the parking lot. "And I know the perfect place."

Chapter 14

#156 Welcome Home.

Kayden

It's taken me a couple of weeks to set it up and even longer to get the balls to go through with it. But after that night I spent with Callie, talking and reliving our past, I knew I had to do it. I have to give Seth most of the credit, for helping me out and for managing to keep it a secret. In the end, it was my speech about how Callie deserved this that won his sworn secrecy over.

I'm nervous the entire drive there, not just because I'm unsure how Callie will react, but because I'm uncertain how *I'll* react. It feels like things are suddenly moving so quickly, not just with our relationship, but also with life. I feel like sometimes I'm running my hardest to keep up with it, except when I'm with Callie. With her, I feel like we're walking through it, enjoying every moment together. And that's how I decided.

It was time.

"Where are we?" she asks, leaning forward to get a

better look at where we are through the veil of snow hitting the window.

I turn off the car and the wipers stop moving, making it even harder for her to see. "It's a surprise."

"At a park?" she questions as she unfastens her seat-belt.

Nodding, I grab the door handle and push it open. "Yeah, follow me."

The park is just part of the surprise. The rest of it is what's in the building right behind the park.

Her perplexity makes this even more entertaining as we get out of the car and she follows me through the snow and around the swing set to the slide. I'm rewarded even more when I start climbing up the ladder and her jaw drops.

"What on earth are you doing?" she asks, dumbfounded, as she watches me climb higher.

I glance over my shoulder down at her. "If you want to find out, you're going to have to follow me."

She eyes the soaking wet ladder with skepticism, but I know she'll do it—she's too brave to let a little wet metal get in her way.

Just like I knew she would, she starts up the ladder. When I reach the top, I hop into the tunnel slide and go down it, getting rewarded by a sopping wet puddle at the bottom and a bump on the head from the to-do list I had

Seth secure in the slide just before we got here.

Okay, maybe it wasn't the best idea to put it there.

Reaching up, I unhook the string securing it in place and remove the small whiteboard. Seth's erased the entire list except for number one hundred fifty-five, which might be my favorite number ever. I tuck the board to my side, face down so the snow doesn't smear the marker.

"You want me to slide down this?" Callie calls down through the slide with bafflement in her voice.

I lower my head into the slide and yell, "Hell yes!"

There's a pause, and then I hear her squeal as she lowers her feet in and slides down.

"Holy crap!" Her ass gets wet when she reaches the bottom and she quickly jumps out of the slide. "That's cold." Once she gets her footing, she looks from me to what's in my hand. "What are you holding?"

"Your surprise." I give the whiteboard over, keeping it face down, but it's more because of my nerves than the fear that it'll get wet and ruined.

She rubs her lips together as she arches her brows at me. "You stole my whiteboard?"

"No. I had Seth borrow it for me." I tap the back of it, noting that there's a slight tremble to my fingers, something I blame on the snow, completely lying to myself.

A cloud of fog encircles her face as she releases a large exhale. Suddenly, she seems nervous, as if she's realized this is no longer a game, but a very serious, life-altering moment.

"I'm afraid to turn it over," she whispers but does it anyway.

I hold my breath as I watch her read the two simple yet very momentous words written in red marker, along with the arrow pointing forward at the apartment complex across from where we're standing. She must read it a few times because it takes a little bit before she looks up at me.

"*Welcome home?*" Her brows dip and her head angles to the side as she glances from me to the board. Then her gaze tracks the direction of where the arrow is pointing. I know the moment it clicks in her head what I'm trying to say with this whole charade because her breath catches.

"You and Seth are always doing crazy things like this whenever you ask me out or try to cheer me up," I tell her then nonchalantly shrug. Her gaze locks on mine and I squirm in my skin. She hasn't shown any signs of being happy, and I'm getting worried that maybe this isn't what she really wanted. "I thought maybe it was my turn"—I brush her hair out of her eyes—"to do something surprising for you."

She's silent for what feels like forever, her eyes never

leaving mine. It's like she's trying to read my mind or see into my soul or something. If anyone could, it'd be Callie. I just wish I could do the same with her right now because her quietness is maddening.

"This is what you want?" She gestures at the board then the apartment without looking away from me.

I nod. "More than anything." But then I hesitate. "Is this what you want, though?"

She assesses me for a moment or two longer like she's searching for a hidden answer inside me. She must find it because suddenly, she's dropping the board onto the ground and throwing her arms around me.

"Of course I want this." She hugs me more tightly than one would expect those thin arms of hers capable of. "I've wanted it for a long time."

I hug her back with everything I have in me. "I think I have too, but I was afraid to admit it to myself… afraid to let myself have something good." I pull back to look her. "Sorry it took me so long. Do you forgive me?"

"There's nothing to forgive." She slips her hand down my arm and threads our fingers, beaming as she looks up at me. "Now, let's go see it."

I scoop up the now soaked whiteboard and lead the way across the park to the sidewalk where we trot up the stairs of building number three. When we reach the second floor, I take the key out of my pocket and nervously unlock the door, fumbling a few times before I finally get it.

"Welcome home," I say then push the door open.

Chapter 15

#156 Welcome Home (Yeah, I know it's the same as #155, but it seemed too epic not to get two numbers. Plus, the first time around, it got erased).

Callie

"It's really small," Kayden tells me as he steps aside to let me enter our apartment. Yes, *our* apartment. "But it's what we can afford, so..." He trails off, ruffling his damp hair into place as he closes the door and shuts out the cold.

"That's okay." I take in the space that I'll now call home. It's not furnished yet so it probably looks bigger than it really is. I'm standing in the living room, which is attached to the dining room/kitchen area and there's a hallway that I assume leads to the bedroom. It's about five times the size of the dorm rooms, which sounds big, but it's really not. I don't care, though. At all. "I could live in a storage room and be okay with it as long as you were there," I tell Kayden. I'm starting to sound like one of those sappy romance books, but oh, well—it seems fitting for the moment.

"So you're okay with it?" Kayden stuffs his hands into the pockets of his jeans, appearing anxious. His brown hair still has drops of snow in it and his cheeks are red from the cold.

I just want to throw my arms around him and hug the crap out of him again.

So I do.

"It's perfect." I squeeze him tightly to show just how happy I am. As his arms circle around me, we share our first hug in our very first home. "But I have to make sure"—I slant back and tip my chin to look at him—"that you're okay with this because we've only been talking about it and then all of a sudden you get a place, and I just want to make sure that it's what you really want because I don't want you to feel pressure or anything. I can wait if I need to."

He snorts a laugh, and when my brows knit, he says, "Sorry. It's just that you kind of sounded like a teenage guy, trying to convince his girlfriend he'll wait to have sex with her."

My cheeks flush. Then I start to think about if he ever used that line on Daisy and my elation sinks. But I realize that it doesn't matter what happened with Daisy because he and I are here and he's mine now, not hers.

"You want to show me the bedroom?" I do my best

come-hither look but it probably comes off more along the lines of seeming confused. At least, that's what I think until his eyes drink me in, and he bites at his bottom lip hard.

"You're starting to get a dirty mind." His smoldering gaze and husky voice sends warm tingles across my skin.

"It must be Seth's influence on me. Sometimes, it's like he's still going through puberty."

Kayden shakes his head, laughing softly under his breath. "All right, no more talking. Let's go show you our bedroom."

We're about halfway across the living room before our lips connect and the clothes start coming off. Shirts are discarded, shoes are kicked off, and we end up leaving a trail of clothing to the bedroom. It's a little chilly in there, but I don't care. Kayden can keep me warm, which is exactly what I tell him as we sink to our knees on the tan carpet and I yank his belt off.

"We should do this every night," he says, unhooking my bra and removing it. "Only in a bed."

"No way. We should totally do it on the floor," I mutter between the kisses he's showering me with on my lips, the arch of my neck, the spot where my heart beats.

He mutters something else, but trails off as my fingers skim down his defined chest to the top of his jeans. Flicking the button undone, I slip my fingers into his boxers and he groans, biting at my flesh.

"Callie..." The sound of my name in the raspy voice he uses causes goose bumps to cover my arms. I become impatient, more than I ever have been before. It's crazy, but the last few weeks have been intense, and I can feel myself changing, becoming more comfortable with myself and who I am with Kayden. So I let my hands wander downward and grasp onto his hardness, something I've never done so boldly before.

"Fuck..." He uses that tone again, and I seriously can't take it anymore. I'm about to rip his jeans off, literally tear the fabric to bits, when I hear a door open and close from somewhere inside the apartment.

We both freeze, panting as we kneel in the center of the room, half naked, our hands grasping at each other.

"Did you hear that?" I whisper, my eyes darting to the door.

Kayden nods, his lips parting, but he's cut off by the sound of a voice.

"Hello, lovebirds," Seth call out. "Are you in here?"

Kayden's and my eyes widen simultaneously. Then we're scrambling to get our clothes, but it's pointless since we both left our shirts and shoes somewhere between the living room and the hallway. My bra is nearby, though, so I get that on while Kayden does up the button of his pants.

"What should we do?" I whisper. "My shirt's out there."

Kayden shrugs, still looking high on the moment. "Ask him to hand the clothes to us."

I wrap my arms around myself. "He'll make a lot of jokes," I warn.

"He's already going to make jokes," Kayden states, giving me a sexy half-smile. "So we might as well go face the music."

"Knock, knock, knock." Seth raps on the shut bedroom door. "Oh, Callie darling, I found something that belongs to you, I think."

"Oh, leave her alone," Greyson says. Then the door cracks and he sticks his arm in with our shirts in his hand. "Here you go guys."

"Thanks, Greyson." I take my shirt and hand Kayden his before I put mine on.

Once we're both dressed, we go out together and face the music.

"What are you doing here?" I ask as we walk into the living room.

Greyson's looking around at our kitchen and Seth is observing the small patio attached to the living room through a sliding glass door.

"I came to see how things went," Seth says, turning to face us. "And to see if you guys wanted to go have dinner and celebrate." He takes in the sight of us; messy hair, wrinkled shirts, and my zippers undone. "But I'm guessing it went well, considering how hot and bothered you two look right now, thanks to my interruption." He flashes me an unapologetic grin.

"We can go," Greyson tells me, taking Seth's hand and yanking him toward the door. Greyson's always been the more levelheaded of the two and tries to keep Seth in line whenever he can. "In fact, we should go and give you two some privacy."

"No, it's okay. We were finished, anyway." I don't mean for it to come out how it sounded, and I feel slightly embarrassed.

"You were?" Kayden cocks an eyebrow at me. "Because I wasn't."

My embarrassment doubles as I playfully swat his arm, hoping it'll divert everyone's attention from my blushing.

"It's okay. We can go get dinner," Kayden says through his chuckles, then his gaze fastens on mine. "*We* can finish later."

While all three of them laugh, I should be even more mortified, but I find myself calmer than anything. Because this is what life is about. Moments like these.

Right now, everything is perfect.

Chapter 16

#103 ~~Outrun~~ Keep Trying to Outrun You Demons.

Kayden

The next day I have a game. I'm excited and nervous and afraid, but that's how it always is for me. There's always a list of things I could mess up on flowing through my head along with a list of things I can do not to fuck up. But sometimes I wish I could get the lists to stop and just play, because I love the game.

I play pretty fucking well through most of the entire game, but only when it veers toward the end does how I perform really matter. The crowd is going wild. Everyone is screaming, hollering, cheering me on, including Callie, Seth, and Greyson, who I know are sitting close to the front, supporting me like they always do. Players are lined up on both sides, me at the back, ready to catch the snap. The lights are bright above me, but a shadow casts over me that no one else can see. We're one touchdown away from winning and there's less than a minute on the clock. The

pressure is on to do well, my teammates, my coach, the entire stadium waiting for me to make the perfect pass. But
it's small in comparison to the voice I hear in my head.

My father's voice.

It's gotten worse since Dylan found him, now a shout
instead of whisper.

Run!

Make the perfect throw!

Win the fucking game!

I hear the snap.

Feel the rush.

You better make this!

It echoes through my head.

I feel the ball touch my hands and I run backwards,
searching for an opening. My heart is pounding in my chest
as players move around the field. I'm aware of them all.
But not as aware as I am of the voice.

You better not fuck this up!

There's no clean throw.

Everyone is covered.

The clock is ticking.

My heart is thrashing.

You better not mess this up!

I scurry to the right, and sprint forward, my feet hammering against the grass as I focus on one thing—outrunning that damn voice. My feet move faster than they ever have before as I dodge to the left. The right. Back and Forth. There are people in front of me, behind me, coming at me from different directions, but my concentration is locked on the end zone. It's all that matters. And as the clock continues to tick with a player grabbing at me from the back, I jump across that line.

Touchdown!

The crowd goes crazy! My team goes crazy! Everyone is running at me. We won! We won! We won!

But I feel like I've lost somehow because in the end I can still hear that damn voice.

You could have done better.

After I'm shower and change, I head out of the locker room even though my team's begging me to go out and celebrate with them.

"Come on, man," Tommy Buliforton says as I sling my bag over my shoulder and walk for the exit door. "You played fucking awesome. We need to go celebrate."

I shake my head. "Nah, I already got other plans," I lie because all I want to do is find Callie and hold her, knowing it'll help me leave the voice of my father behind.

"For someone who made the winning touchdown, you look super fucking depressed," Luke Price says as he follows me out of the locker room while zipping up his coat. Luke's been my best friend since we were kids and has his own problems with his parents. We don't talk about our problems with each other though. I think he saves it for his girlfriend, Violet, just like I do with Callie.

"You're not going out either?" I ask as we step outside and into the cold night.

He shrugs as he searches for Violet in the crowd. "Partying isn't—or can't be my thing anymore, being a recovering alcoholic and all."

"You doing okay with that?" I tug my fingers through my damp hair as I make my way through the people, looking for Callie.

"Yeah, but I know myself enough to know that I'll be doing okay as long as I go home and not out." Luke grins as he spots Violet leaning against a post not too far away from where we are. It's funny, but he never really smiles except for when he's with her.

I wonder if it's the same for me when I'm with Callie?

As if to answer my own question, Callie emerges from the crowd, shoving her way out of the last of the people and a big smile rises on my face.

"Hey you," she says, rushing up to me as some guy hoots and hollers from the crowd. "You played great."

"Yeah… I could have done a little better, though." I wrap my arms around her when she reaches me and pull her against me. Her warmth spreads across my body and I breathe in the serenity of it.

"You did perfect," she whispers in my ear and then leans back. "We should celebrate."

"I did okay," I press. "Not perfect."

Her lips curve to a frown. "No sulking or I'll have to force you to do fun things until you're laughing so hard you pee you pants."

I laugh at her, grazing the pad of my thumb across her bottom lip. "Alright, you win," I say. "I played perfect."

Her lips turn back upward and the sparkle in her eyes matches the stars above us. "You fucking kicked ass."

I can't help myself. I bust up laughing. Callie rarely swears so when she does, it's hilarious. "Oh my God," I say through my laughter. "It's so funny when you say fuck."

She grins, but her cheeks turn a shade of pink. "I knew that one would get you to laugh."

"You always manage to," I say, no longer finding our conversation funny but personal and intimate. "And actually I was thinking we could pick up some takeout and then go hangout at our place."

"Our place." She lets the word roll slowly off her tongue. "That sounds like a great idea to me."

"But if that's okay with you, maybe Luke and Violet could come hang." I glance over at the two of them chatting near the front of the crowd. "It might be nice now that you and Violet are getting along."

Callie nods. "Sounds perfect." She laces her fingers through mine and we walk away from the stadium—away from my father's voice—and by the time we reach my car, it's disappeared completely.

I just wish it would stay that way.

Chapter 17

#157 Get to Know Your Family, Even When It Seems Impossible.

Kayden

Callie and I managed to move in a few things before we had to part ways for Thanksgiving, but between work and school, we still have a ways to go. We did get to spend one night in our apartment together, cuddled up on a blanket and watching movies on my laptop, before she dropped me off at the airport so I could fly out to Virginia for Thanksgiving.

I'm not happy about spending the holiday without her, but I understand she needs to go home and see her brother while I need to go see mine. It's part of growing and getting better, I guess—learning how to do things on my own. I just wish doing things on my own meant I could still hold Callie's hand because it feels weird without her near me.

Dylan's wife—who insists I call her Liz instead of by

her full name, Elizabeth—is freaking out while she tries to get the house in order for her parent's arrival. She's attempting to cook everything all at once and the kitchen smells like burnt toast, the air is heavy with smoke, causing the smoke detectors to sporadically go off.

"Does she need help?" I ask Dylan. We're sitting at the table, playing cards, which blows my freaking mind because it's so normal. It makes me uncomfortable since I'm not used to it. What I'm used to—at least, the last time I was at a family event—is yelling, fighting, hitting, and breaking.

Dylan evaluates his cards as he swallows a gulp of beer. "You can ask her, but she'll flip out on you." He sets two cards face down on the table and takes two more from the deck. Dylan looks a lot like me; brown hair, tall with a medium build, and he's probably my future. Well, except the whole teaching thing. I can't see myself doing that. Honestly, I'm not sure I can picture myself doing this either, sitting at the table while Callie cooks dinner. It seems so rude to make her do it. Plus, Callie doesn't like to cook very much.

"Do you need any help?" I finally ask as Liz rushes back and forth between the stove and a bowl she's been mixing something in.

She's got short blonde hair, blue eyes, and is wearing

an apron over her jeans and T-shirt. She waves me off, scurrying for a towel when she spills milk on the counter. "No. You're the guest and should sit back and relax."

Dylan chuckles under his breath as he rearranges the cards in his hand. "Don't worry. She's going to give up here in about a half an hour, and we'll end up going out."

"So, this is your tradition?" I examine my cards. I don't have a very good hand, but we're not playing for money, just fun. I know why, too. When we were younger, our father would make us play for money. If he won, he'd take all his winnings, and if he lost, he'd beat the shit out of us because in his words, "we were cheating bastards." So, really, we'd always lose.

Dylan nods, laying his cards down, and I do the same. I think I like Dylan a little bit more when instead of bragging about winning, he says, "Yeah, if she'd just let me help though, it wouldn't be a problem. I'm an excellent cook."

As Liz whisks by the table, she whips Dylan in the side with the dish towel she's carrying. "That's such a lie. You equally suck at cooking, which is why we have at least five takeout places on speed dial."

"One for each weekday?" I joke, gathering the cards.

Liz nods with a serious expression, and it makes me

166

smile that they have their own thing going here, one that doesn't seem at all like my parents. They're not nasty to each other. They smile. Laugh. Seem happy.

It's nice and kind of a relief because it gives me the tiniest ray of hope that I won't turn out like my father, that I can have this normalcy, happiness, that I can have a future filled with what I want and with who I want.

"You want to go watch the game?" Dylan asks, nodding at the living room as he picks up his beer and scoots his chair back from the table.

"Sure." I get up and we wander into the living room and settle on the leather couch in front of the flat screen. The maroon walls are decorated with photos of the two of them—at their wedding, the beach, on the top of a mountain. It makes me sad because I don't have any photos where I look happy. Callie and I don't even have any photos of us on the wall.

"So, you think you're ever going to do this?" Dylan asks after we sit in silence through a couple of plays.

"Do what?" I ask, tipping my head back to sip my soda.

He picks at the damp label on the beer bottle. "Play professionally…" He leans forward to set the beer on the coffee table then faces me, resting against the armrest. "Liz says you're pretty good."

I thrum my fingers against the side of the soda can, a pucker forming at my brow. "When has she seen me play?"

"She watches your games on the internet."

"All of them?" I'm dumbfounded. She watches me play? Really? Why?

"Most of them," he says. "And I've watched a few, too. I'd watch more, but I'm working on getting my master's degree right now, so I don't have a lot of free time." He pats me on the arm. "Don't look so surprised. We care about you, Kayden." Abruptly, the mood shifts and takes on a more serious tone. "I know it might seem like I don't since we didn't talk for years, but if I would have known what was going on in that house... that he'd gotten *that* bad... that he would actually try... " He can't even get the words out, and he ends up giving up. "I wouldn't have been absent for so long. I shouldn't have, and it's one of my biggest regrets."

"I kind of understand why you did it, though." I stare at the soda in my hand. "I had a hard time just coming here... The whole family thing is strange to me because it's good, yet it reminds me of how bad things can be. And I don't mean you. You were never bad. And Tyler, well, he was great until he started doing drugs and turned into a mess. But I mean Mom and Dad."

Dylan reaches for his beer. "It is hard, isn't it? It took me forever to figure out how to be in a house with Liz, how to act like a family because I didn't have a freaking clue. I felt so lost, you know?"

"And now? Is it better now...? Because it seems like it is."

"Yeah, now I'm happy." He offers me a small smile then takes a sip of the beer before he asks, "So what about you, Kayden? Are you happy?"

I half shrug. "Sure. I guess"

His cheeriness deflates. "You guess?"

I shrug again. "Sometimes I am, but I wish I could figure out how to be all the time, you know." He looks upset so I explain further. "It's just that I have no idea what I want to do with my life... I mean, football's great and I'm good at it and enjoy playing it, but I only got into it because of dad. And that's the thing. It all..." I release a loud breath. "It all comes back to him. I don't want to have anything to do with him and every time something is connected to him, I'm not happy... I swear to God, I can sometimes hear his voice in my head when I'm out playing... I just want to be able to play for me..." I cease talking, unsure why I decided to say all that aloud when I haven't even told Callie about that yet.

169

Dylan's shoulders slump, maybe from the weight of the memories of my father. "Kayden, you shouldn't let that… *him* stop you from doing anything. It only gives him that much more power over your life. If playing football makes you happy, then do it. I know it's hard, but you need to let this thing with Dad go—let the past go. And I think once you do, you'll stop hearing all that fucked up shit he said to you all the time—you'll be able to play for you."

"You pretty much just stated word for word what my therapist said," I tell him then sigh heavily. "And I know I should… and I'm trying to. It's just going to take some time for me to figure shit out." I set the can down on the end table, then cross my arms as I recline in the sofa, wondering if there will ever be a time I can play for me and just love the game. I sure as hell hope so. "I have a ways to go though… I mean, I still fuck up sometimes with certain things." I'm not going to go any further than that, not ready to discuss my cutting disorder with him.

"Everyone does that. It's called life, Kayden."

"Yeah, I know."

As gap of silence goes by, I start to focus back on the game. Someone just scored a touchdown and the crowd is going crazy. The sight puts me in a state of contentment, like it does for me whenever I'm playing.

"What about girl you're dating?" he asks, drawing my attention back to him. "Are you still seeing her?"

"Callie?" I extend my arm to grab my soda. "Yeah, we actually just got our own place right before I headed out here."

His eyes widen in astonishment. "Shut the fuck up. Seriously?" he asks and I nod, caught off guard by his excitement. "Wow, I didn't know you guys were that serious. You never really seemed like you were on the phone. Then again, you barely talk about your private life, either, so…" he trails off sadly.

"Don't take that personally," I tell him. "I only talk about that stuff with Callie."

He nods, relaxing. "Wow, you are fucking serious with this girl, aren't you?"

"Who's serious with a girl?" Liz interrupts our conversation as she comes strolling in with a plate of what looks like burnt squash. I didn't even know you could burn squash.

"Kayden," Dylan tells her at the same time I say, "No one."

Dylan's grin is conniving as he glances from me to Liz. "Callie and Kayden moved in together."

"Really?" Her eyes light up as she sets the plate down on the coffee table in front of us. "That's so huge, Kayden.

Why didn't you tell us?"

Again, Dylan appears a bit hurt, and it makes me feel sort of remorseful. Maybe I've been going about this whole getting-to-know-your-family thing all wrong. Maybe I shouldn't have been shutting them out as much as I have. But it's difficult to let people in when I know how bad they can hurt me. Still, I decide to try because, if Callie were here, that's what she'd want me to do.

"Sorry, I think it just slipped my mind," I say apologetically. "I'm not used to telling people things, I guess."

"Well, that I do get." Dylan nervously cracks his knuckles. "I've actually been needing to talk to you about something."

I can tell by his sullen tone what it's pertaining to. "You found out more about our parents, didn't you?"

"I got a call from Mom this morning, but I've been procrastinating telling you because I didn't want to ruin the trip. But I guess we're never going to have much of a relationship if we don't start talking to each other, are we?" he asks, and even though I'm not too thrilled to hear more about Mom and Dad, I nod. He wavers, uncertainty filling his expression. "She actually wanted to tell me about our father." Another long pause as he squirms in the chair. "It's bad, Kayden. Dad, I mean… He's in bad shape."

I'm fairly sure an entire set of commercials plays before I'm able to get ahold of my voice and emotions enough to respond. "How bad?"

Resolution.

This is what you wanted, right?

You are a terrible person.

Dylan lets out an exhausted breath. "Really, really bad."

It's strange, but it seems like we should be crying or something, yet our eyes are dry. My heart feels the same way too, and those thoughts of how I've got to be a bad person come rushing back to me. This can't be normal—to feel nothing toward the person that raised you. Regardless, that's how I feel.

Absolutely nothing.

"I think he's going to die," Dylan says quietly.

And again, *nothing.*

I think Callie might have been wrong because there's no way I'm not broken.

Chapter 18
#159 Don't Panic When Things Get Brutally Ugly.

Callie

It's the day after Thanksgiving, and the house I grew up in is already sparkling with Christmas lights. There's a large pine tree in need of decorating and tons of cut out snowflakes waiting to be hung up. My mother is one of those people who *loves* the holidays to the point where it might be an unhealthy obsession. However, after years and years of it, my brother, father, and I have learned to tolerate it. We've also learned how to avoid countless hours of trimming the tree with silver ornaments and tinsel.

"I can't believe she bought your lie this time," my brother Jackson states from the front seat of my father's truck as he fidgets with the stereo. "Telling her we're going to buy some replacement bulbs for the lights, even though all of them are up. I still can't believe you actually took a couple of the bulbs out so some wouldn't work."

Jackson looks better than he used to; less stoner/pothead and more hipster. He's been attending community college in Florida where my grandparents live and he works as a manager at an electronic store. I'm glad to see him like this instead of the druggie jerk he was when he spent so much time with Caleb.

My father chuckles as he turns the wipers up a notch. "I've been having to get more creative with my excuses to get out of the house. Picking up Callie was a long one." He grins at me from over his shoulder. "And a good one, too."

I smile back then watch the snowflakes splatter against the window. The snow hasn't let up since he picked me up from Laramie three days ago. No one I knew was going that way, and Kayden was worried his car wasn't safe enough to get me there with how bad the roads have been. When I told my dad this, he not only got excited to come pick me up, but he also remarked what a great guy Kayden is for thinking of my safety.

"You've been awfully quiet," my father says as he makes a right onto Main Street.

"That's because she's lovesick." Jackson smirks at me, and I stick out my tongue.

"Is that what it is?" my father asks, and I vow to get Jackson back for bringing this up. "Do you miss Kayden?"

"Of course I miss him," I say, unzipping my coat because Jackson is overheating the car with how high he's got the heater turned up. "But I'm always this quiet."

175

"That's true," Jackson mumbles. He folds his arms and stares out the window at the buildings bordering the street. The town is small, but it's the day after Thanksgiving and the sales the stores are having is causing havoc in the streets.

"We should go snowboarding or something this weekend," Jackson suddenly says to me. I know what he's doing. Ever since I told my family about what happened with Caleb, Jackson has acted almost too nice. I think he feels guilty because Caleb was his friend, and therefore, was in the house because of him. I don't blame Jackson for what happened, though. It's not like he knew it was going to happen. Caleb had everyone fooled.

"I don't really know how to snowboard," I admit as our dad turns into the busy parking lot of the hardware store located in the heart of the town. "And I don't have a board."

"You can borrow my old one. And we'll go down the small hill."

I frown. "You mean, the bunny hill?"

He unclicks his seatbelt. "See, you already know the lingo. You'll be fine."

I roll my eyes but agree to go. Then the three of us hop out of the car and face the madness of the store. There's so many people there we have to stand in a line just to get inside.

"Wow, people are crazy," Jackson mumbles, tugging the hood of his coat over his head as we wait to get in the doors. "You should have thought of something else, Dad, that didn't require going into stores."

"Yeah, you're probably right," my dad agrees, putting on a pair of gloves. "But I panicked when you mother came at me with the inflatable Santa."

I'm laughing at him when my phone vibrates from inside my pocket. I take it out as we move forward with the line, already guessing who the text is from.

And I'm right.

Kayden: So how's it going?

Me: Super great except for the whole avoid-crazy-mom thing turned into an enter-crazy-shopper thing.

Kayden: ???

Me: My dad makes up an excuse every year to get us out of the house while my mother goes mad ninja Christmas crazy on the house. But this time he didn't put enough thought into it because he took us to the store. And people are nuts. There's a line just to get into the store.

Kayden: I'm sorry you're not having fun :(

Me: I actually am. It's good to see my dad and

Jackson... he actually offered to take me snowboarding this weekend.

Kayden: U should go. It's a lot of fun.

Me: I told him I would, but I'm pretty sure I'll just spend the day falling on my butt.

Kayden: At least you'll look adorable doing it ;)

Me: Hmm... I'm not so sure. I think my adorableness is only seen by your eyes.

Kayden: No way. U just don't see it.

I'm about to text back when I realize Jackson and my dad are staring at me with silly grins on their faces.

"What?" I ask them.

Jackson sniggers, shaking his head, while my dad just continues to smile. "It's nothing." He turns and moves forward with the line. "How's Kayden doing?"

"Good. But how'd you know I was texting him?" I wonder, pulling my hood over my head as the wind picks up.

"Because you have that lovesick, puppy dog look in your eyes," Jackson says smugly as we finally, FINALLY make it into the store.

"I do not," I protest as another text comes through my phone. I have to keep my elbows tucked in while I type just to avoid getting slammed into.

Kayden: U still there?

Me: Yeah, my dad and Jackson interrupted me. Sorry.

Kayden: So other than shopping, how's your day going?

My dad takes one look at the congested aisles and then gives a loud clap of his hands. "All right, who's ready for this?" When neither Jackson nor I respond, he claps his hands again then leans down like we're in a huddle. "All right, Jackson. You go up the left aisle and to the back to get the bulbs. Callie, I'm out of staples, too, so you go right and about halfway to the back of the store then make another right. I'll go get in line and save us a spot so we're not waiting all day." He claps his hands for a third time then says, "Break."

Jackson and I trade an oh-my-God look because we're so used to this. Growing up with a father who's a high school football coach, everything's about the game. Still, we head off to our designated areas, splitting apart and shoving our way through the crazed shoppers. As I make my way to the aisle, I text Kayden back.

Me: Good. Nothing too exciting is going on. Well, except for the fact that my dad just made Jackson and I huddle up so he could give as a play by play of how we were going to get through the store.

179

Kayden: Must be the coach in him.

Me: I guess so. Or that he's just getting crazier with old age.

Kayden: God, I wish I could be there. I miss u so fucking bad.

Me: I miss you too. Is everything ok?

Kayden: Yeah. Actually things are good. Liz ended up burning the dinner, but we ate at this really nice place. And Dylan and I have been talking a lot. I even got to see Tyler for a day, and he seemed a lot better.

Me: What about your parents? Have u heard anything more?

It takes him a little while to answer. By the time the text comes through, I've made it to the shelf with a small selection of staples on it.

Kayden: Yeah. Dylan talked to my mom a little bit yesterday. My dad's in really bad shape. Not sure if he's going to make it. My mother's still not saying how he got there in the first place. But I found out they're in North Carolina.

I'm shocked. Not going to make it? Oh my God, how do I even respond to that? Normally, I'd feel really sorry, but I know from the conversation I had with Kayden in the car that his feelings about all this are buried in confusion created by years of physical abuse.

Me: I'm so sorry. Do u want me to call u when I get out of the store?

I grab a box of staples and turn to leave the aisle, ready to get out of there so I can hear well enough to call Kayden and make sure he's doing okay. I'm distracted by my phone, not paying attention to where I'm going, and I end up slamming into someone.

The box of staples and my phone slip from my fingers. "Shit," I curse, bending down to pick them up. "Sorry about that."

"Don't worry about it."

The sound of the voice sends the hairs on the back of my neck on end. I haven't heard that voice in over a year. It's a voice I wish I'd never heard to begin with, wish to God I wasn't hearing now.

"Fuck," I mutter under my breath, scrambling to pick up my phone and the staples without looking up at Caleb. *He can't be here. He can't be here.*

He just can't.

But he is, something I painfully have to acknowledge after I collect my stuff and stand back up. He's right in front of me, wearing that stupid look on his face, the one that says he thinks he has control over me.

But he doesn't anymore.

I do.

"What the fuck are you doing here?" I'm surprised at how steady my voice is. I make myself carry his gaze, but those dark eyes of his are still difficult to look at it.

"Wow, you've developed quite the mouth on you," he says. He looks rundown; bags under his eyes, holes in his jeans, and the oversized coat he's wearing nearly swallows his thin body. This isn't the Caleb I used to know, but he still sends my heart racing with fear. "That's two fucks and a shit that's left your lips in the last minute. The Callie I used to know couldn't even say crap without getting flustered."

"The Callie you knew doesn't exist anymore." I suck in a breath, feeling my heart tremble in my chest. "And honestly, you never really knew her."

"Didn't I?" His gaze flicks across my body. I'm not wearing anything revealing—jeans, a coat, and boots—but suddenly, I feel like I'm standing in front of him with my Halloween costume on, vulnerable, as if he's seeing all of me. And it's not for him to see. Ever again!

"I'm leaving." I dodge to the side to swing around him. I'll go find my dad and Jackson where I know I'll be safe and then call the cops. Caleb violated his probation when he skipped town after drug charges were pressed against him, so he's in trouble. I just wish it was for what he did to me.

Before I can skitter around him, he shuffles to the side and blocks my path. There are a couple of people nearby, but they're too preoccupied by bright neon sale stickers to notice what's going on. Or they're just too afraid to do intervene.

"Relax, Callie. I just want to talk." His lips curl to a smirk, revealing the monster side of him. This is what he's always done to me, tried to torture me and get under my skin just by looking at me. I think he actually enjoys seeing me panic, but I'm not going to give him the satisfaction of it like I used to.

Standing up straight, I turn to head in the opposite direction. But things get brutally ugly as he snatches hold of my arm and his fingers dig through the fabric of my coat. A fire and a chill whirl through me simultaneously, the chill stemming from my fear, but the fire giving me anger, giving me strength.

Without even flinching, I whirl around and shove him back with the pent up rage of the last seven years. "Don't fucking touch me." My voice is calm yet firm as he stumbles back in shock. I don't wait for him to say anything because I don't care what he has to say.

Nothing that he does matters.

He's not part of my life anymore.

I'm in control.

I am strong.

Still, by the time I make it to my dad and Jackson, I'm on the verge of crying. Not because I'm afraid, but because I'm so angry.

"Shit, Callie. What's wrong?" Jackson asks as I rush up to them.

"Call the police. Tell them Caleb's here," I say, wiping my tears away with the back of my hand. People are staring at me like I'm insane, but right now I don't care. I just care about getting out of this store.

"Did he hurt you?" Jackson asks then takes off in the direction I just came from without waiting for my response. "I'm going to beat his ass."

I snag the sleeve of his coat before he can get too far. "He didn't hurt me. Just call the police, okay? It's way better than beating his ass and then you getting in trouble for it."

He glances back and forth between the aisles and me with confliction. Eventually, he gives in. "Fine." He retrieves his phone, muttering, "Dumb fuck must be hiding out at his parents' house." He storms off toward the doors, shoving people out of his way as he puts the phone up to his ear.

I try to breathe quietly, but I start to struggle for air. I keep scanning the store for signs of Caleb, waiting for him to appear again.

Finally, my dad removes the staples from my quivering hand and sets them and the bulbs down on the nearest rack. "We can wait to get those," he says then puts an arm around me and steers me out the doors to the truck, even though I can tell that, like Jackson, he wants to turn around and beat the crap out of Caleb.

He asks me a thousand times if I'm okay. Jackson does the same thing when he gets off the phone. I keep telling them yes because I really am okay. Yeah, Caleb is a horrible person who did horrible things, but I finally stood up for myself. I didn't panic, didn't let him win.

It's taken me seven years to get to this place, and even though I'm still terrified, I'm also strong. Stronger than I used to be.

Stronger than the monster.

Chapter 19
#160 Get To Her—Get Home No Matter What.

Kayden

It's the day after Thanksgiving, and I'm sitting on the sofa, watching some television with Dylan and Liz while I text Callie during the commercials. It's been both a rough and decent day as Dylan and I all struggle through our feelings about my dad being in a coma while trying to enjoy each other's company. I don't think any of us knows what to do with the information about my father, so we've all sort of been quiet, afraid to be the first one to speak, to say what we're all thinking—that we might not be as upset as we should be. I could see it in Dylan's eyes the more we talked and in Tyler's eyes too, which were less hazy than the last time I saw him. We didn't get to visit him for too long, but it was nice to see him while he wasn't high out of his mind. He kind of reminded me of the Tyler I knew who taught me how to ride a bike, not the one who took off to become a drug addict and left me behind.

"I'm going to go make some popcorn," Liz announces

during a commercial as she stands up from the couch. "Kayden, do you need anything?"

I shake my head. "No, I'm good." I pull out my phone and text Callie again. She hasn't responded to my last two texts, and I'm starting to wonder what's up. It's making me uneasy, but that feeling could also be stemming from the fact that I'm under a lot of emotional stress and haven't picked up a razor yet.

Kayden: Hey, it's me again. R u okay? I'm starting to get worried.

I hold my phone for a while, waiting for a text to come through, but instead it starts to ring. Callie's name flashes across the screen and a smile touches my lips as I get up and go back to the guestroom where I've been spending my nights.

"I'm glad you called," I say, shutting the door behind me. I don't bother turning the lamp on since there's still enough sunlight to light up the room. "I was starting to get a little worried."

"I know you were," she replies apologetically. "Sorry. I should have called sooner." Her voice carries an edge and I know right away that something's not right.

"Something is wrong"—I shove some of my dirty clothes out of the way then lie down on the bed—"isn't there?"

She lets out a shaky breath. "Kind of. I mean, every-thing's okay now."

My body goes rigid. "But it wasn't a while ago?"

"No, not really."

I hesitate, unsure if I should ask because of her reluc-tant tone. "Do you...? Do you want to talk about it?"

"Not really," she sighs. "But I probably should." An-other sigh. Then another. It's driving me crazy knowing something happened, but not knowing exactly what. "I ran into Caleb today." Her voice is barely a whisper.

I bolt upright from the bed, completely taken off guard. "What? Where?" As my hands ball into fists, I have to stab my nails into my palms to keep myself from losing it. I need to calm down. Need to de-stress somehow because I'm feeling that pull again toward my razor... my flesh... the pain... the blood... the relief. I squeeze my eyes shut. "Please, tell me you're okay."

"I'm fine, Kayden. I promise. I just ran into him at the store while I was texting you. It's why I stopped." Her pause lasts forever. "I'm okay, though. I totally stood up to him and even shoved him when he tried to grab me."

"He tried to grab you?" I'm so furious I have to pry my nails away from my palms and grab onto a nearby throw pillow to grip the shit out of it. "In a fucking store?"

"Yes, but it's okay," Callie says quickly. "I got to stand up to him like I've always wanted to do. And Jackson called the cops and they arrested him. God, I can't believe he's behind bars." She sounds happy about it, but I'm still stuck on the part where he put his freaking hands on her.

"I want to beat the shit out of him right now," I admit, chucking the pillow at the wall, "for touching you."

"But you don't need to this time," she states proudly. "I took care of him myself. I stood up to him and Jackson called the police, and he was arrested for the drug charges pressed against him last year, so he might end up in jail. And I know that it in no way makes up for what he did to me, but it still feels like I'm getting a little bit of resolution."

"Callie..." I struggle with what to say, with what to do, with how to calm myself down and not have another slip up.

"Kayden..." Her tone is lighter than one would expect it to be. How can she be so calm while I'm a wreck? And it doesn't even have anything to do with me.

"Tell me what to do," I say in a strained whisper. "I need to do something; otherwise, I'm going to lose it."

"You can tell me about how you are," she suggests. "I need a distraction."

"Really? That's all you need?"

"Yes."

"I can do that." I exhale then try to relax and tell her about my trip, even though I've already texted her about the majority of it. But she asked me to do it and that's all that really matters. Not *my* need to beat Caleb or *my* rage. It's not about *me*, but about *her*.

After I've yammered her ear off for about an hour, long enough that the sun is gradually descending behind the mountains, I stop to give her some time to speak, asking her what her plans are, besides snowboarding with her brother.

"Well, I should probably tell you I'm heading back to Laramie tomorrow morning," she tells me, and I can hear her typing on her computer, probably either writing a story for a class or an article for her internship.

"But I thought you weren't going back until Monday morning?" I slip my shoes off and kick them off the bed.

"Yeah, but Jackson wants me to show him all the fun partying stuff to do in Laramie on Saturday and then hit some slopes down there on Sunday. Honestly, I'm ready to get out of this town. As much fun as I've had decking out the Christmas tree, I miss our home."

I smile as I lean against the headboard and stretch out my legs. "I miss our home too, but I have to ask, *you're* showing *Jackson* the party scene? Really?"

When she laughs, it's the most serene sound I've ever heard, like what music does to some people. "Yeah, crazy, right? I'd worry I'd disappoint, but he seems to have chilled out on the partying, and I think it's been a while, so I'm hoping that means it won't take a lot for him to have fun. Plus, Luke and Violet are there."

I can't contain my laughter. "So you, Luke, Violet, and Jackson are all going to hang out?"

"Hey, I'm friends with them too," she protests. "And I already texted Luke to tell him what's up, and he said he was down to chill as long as it's low key."

"I know you're friends with them." I let my laughter die down. "Sorry, it was just a little unexpected. I'm sure you'll have fun, although I'm jealous I can't be there."

"I'm sorry you can't, but I'm totally going to have fun," she says mischievously. "I'm going to wear that dress I wore on Halloween and be a party animal."

"No way. No wearing that dress without me around."

"You sound jealous."

"I am."

"You should come home early then, and I'll put on the dress for you." She pauses. "Or maybe I'll just wear the boots and nothing else."

I bite down on my lip hard, a growl rising in my throat.

"Are you trying to entice me with your sexiness?"

"Maybe." The naughtiness in her voice is making me go rock hard. "Is it working?"

I have to adjust myself as I picture her in what she's describing. "Fuck, yeah. I'm hard as hell."

I hear her breath catch and can picture her blushing. "So do you think you can swing it?"

"Doing you in those boots?" I ask. "Hell, yeah."

She snorts a laugh. "No. I mean come home early."

God, what I wouldn't give to be home with her, especially after what happened with Caleb. Regardless if she says she's okay, I still need to see for myself—need to be there for her. But how?

"I wish I could, but I'm not sure I could afford to switch flights." I sigh. It's not like I want to get away from my brother. I just miss Callie. Things are starting to get to me here, and I know if I was with her, it wouldn't be as hard to deal with.

"Yeah, I know. You probably shouldn't either. I was just being selfish."

"You weren't being selfish. You're allowed to want me."

Her soft laughter vibrates through my ear and makes me want to be near her even more. "Well, I want you all the

time, but I guess, if I have to, I can wait until Monday."
She pauses, and I hear someone saying something. "Sorry,
but I have to go. My mom wants me to come help her bake
pies." She sounds less than thrilled about it.

"Have fun," I tease because I know she hates baking.

"Ha, ha." She doesn't find me funny at all. "I love
you."

My heart swells inside my chest. Those words will
never get old. I want to hear them in person where I can
kiss her right after they're uttered. "I love you, too."

The silence gets to me the moment I hang up as my
problems come rushing back to me. I feel so alone, so confused, so in need to see Callie, just to make sure she's okay.
I'm tempted to do things to get my mind off the emotional
overload. There are only two things I feel like doing right
now—seeing Callie and picking up my razor. And one
seems so much easier to do at the moment than the other.

Chapter 20

#161 Go Home When You Need to. There's No Shame in Leaving Early.

Kayden

I can't shake the feeling that things are about to change. That something bad is about to happen. Call it years of getting these feelings right before my father would get set off. I guess he somehow built an alarm inside me.

For the most part, the day is going good. We're sitting around, playing Scrabble, laughing about the perverted word my brother just laid down and got forty-something points for—cock.

"God, I feel like I'm married to a teenage boy," Liz remarks, throwing a tile at Dylan who laughs when it pegs him in the forehead.

"You like my dirty mind," he replies. "Don't lie."

She's about to snap a comeback when Dylan's phone rings.

And we all just sort of freeze.

I'm not even sure why we do. It's not like we know

who's calling, or maybe we do. Maybe there's some sort of silent forewarning we all picked up on, like the alarm inside me.

I can tell Dylan doesn't want to answer it, but he does anyway. And within thirty seconds, his skin pales and he looks ill.

Whatever it is, it is bad.

He seems lost for words, tugging his fingers through his hair as he nods and slumps back in his chair. "Uh. Okay."

I'm watching him like a hawk, waiting for him to show a sign that will let me know what the fuck is going on.

"Kayden, why don't you come help me move the sofa?" Liz suddenly says, pushing back from the table. "I've been dying to rearrange the living room and could use an extra pair of strong arms."

I don't bother pointing out that it'd be easier if Dylan and I moved it because it really isn't about that but about getting me out of the kitchen and away from Dylan and the phone call.

"Okay…" I hesitantly get up from the table and follow her out of the kitchen and into the living room.

"So how are you doing?" she asks as I reach down to grab the side of the sofa.

"Good, I guess." I throw a glance over my shoulder to

the kitchen before I raise my side of the sofa, intentionally bearing most of the weight because, like Callie, Liz is short and slender. But she seems to hold her own as she lifts her side with almost the same ease as me.

"Just good?" she question as she spins us in the opposite direction.

I shrug after we set the sofa down. "It's been fun visiting you guys."

She wipes the sweat from her brow. "I don't mean with this trip," she says. "I mean this thing with your mom and dad."

I'm not sure how to respond, and thankfully I don't have to because Dylan comes walking into the living room. He has his hand covering the receiver of the phone. "Um..." he struggles, "she wants to talk to you."

He doesn't have to say who *she* is. I know it's my mother, and I jerk back like he hit me. "N-no," I stammer. "I don't want to talk to her."

He appears torn on how to reply, but I think it's because arguing with my mom is the worst thing possible since, in her eyes, she's always right.

"Dylan, you shouldn't even ask him," Liz hisses. "Just tell her no."

Dylan blinks like he's snapped out of a trance then

quickly puts the phone up to his ear. "He's not going to talk to you," he says.

I'm not sure what my mother says to Dylan, but his shoulders look heavier with each second that ticks by. When he finally hangs up, he looks hunched over old man as he slumps onto the sofa Liz and I just moved. He lowers his head into his hands and presses his palms to his eyes.

"What did the evil bitch want now?" Liz asks, sitting by Dylan. I decide right then and there that I like Liz.

"She wanted to tell us that"—Dylan elevates his head and looks at me—"Dad's probably not going to make it through the next week." As he presses his lips together, I can't tell whether he's upset about Dad or having to talk to Mom. "She wants us to come to North Caroline and say our good-byes."

I swiftly shake my head, flexing my fingers, fighting the urge to pierce my nails into my flesh. "No, I can't do that."

"I know you can't." Dylan's expression softens. "And that's exactly what I told her."

My muscles unravel the slightest bit. "What about you? Are you... going to?"

Liz looks about as eager to hear Dylan's answer as I do.

"No," he says firmly. "I said my good-byes the day I

turned eighteen."

Shutting my eyes, I nod. I feel like I'm on the verge of crying, thinking about how I never did get to say good-bye. That the last real exchange I had was with my father was when he looked down at me with hate in his eyes as I bled out on the kitchen floor. I wonder if he thought I was going to die. I wonder if he was happy because of it. I want to stop wondering about all this. I want to say good-bye like Dylan did, but not to my dad, to the past. And I want to go to my future.

"I need to go home." I don't mean to say it aloud, but the moment I do is the moment I realize just how much I need to.

Thankfully, Dylan sees it too, because he stands up and crosses the room, giving me a weird, awkward but welcomed hug. "I know you do. And I think I have an idea."

Chapter 21

#162 Have a Mad, Crazy Snowball Fight.

Callie

Before Jackson and I head to Laramie, he and my dad load up the truck with some furniture my mom decided to give me that was in the guestroom—the one that still isn't finished. It consists of a queen size bedframe and mattress, a dresser and nightstand along with a couple of barstools for the kitchen. She also throws in some of her old cooking supplies even though I tell her I don't like to cook. I think I actually break her heart when I say that, but I also break it earlier when I told her I was leaving early.

She cries the entire time she's hugging me good-bye and then while Jackson and I are pulling out of the driveway.

"Thank God that's over," Jackson remarks as he drives toward Laramie. He'll only be visiting for two days, but he keeps insisting we're going to, *"Snowboard like pros and party like rock stars"* while he's there.

"She means well," I say, taking my laptop out of a bag

199

to get some work done for my internship because I haven't done anything since Thanksgiving break started.

"She may *mean* well," he replies as he pulls into a gas station so he can fill up the tank before we hit the highway, "but she comes off crazy."

I laugh yet don't go too much further into the making-fun-of-mom. She may be intense, but deep down, I do believe she means well and that the extremely overbearing attitude she's had lately is coming from what happened to me. I think she feels like she needs to make up for what happened by smothering me. And instead of fighting her, I've decided to let her be. Of course, telling my brother this will only get me teasing remarks about being a mama's girl.

When Jackson gets out to put gas in the truck, I get situated in the backseat with my laptop on my lap. But five minutes later when he gets back in and starts driving again, I'm still staring at that damn cursor. I swear it's begging me to write something else. Even though I know I shouldn't, I end up switching to my fiction yet kind of non-fiction story, and suddenly, my fingers come alive.

This monster wasn't in disguise like the one the girl had met so many years ago. He snarled his fangs and raised his fists, ready to break everything in his path.

Knowing that she would only get one chance with this, the girl rushed forward before she could back out.

"Stop." Her voice was as small as she felt, and when the monster turned to look at her, she wanted to run, but honestly, she was sick of running, so tired of monsters winning.

"Can I help you?" the monster asked, his fangs disappearing, his eyes softening as he shape-shifted into his misleading form. He thought the girl couldn't see anymore what lay beneath the disguise, but she could.

See.

The monster.

In his eyes.

"You're needed inside," the girl lied, her voice surprisingly steady and her feet firmly planted to the ground. She glanced at the boy, who was standing so still she thought he might be frozen.

The monster looked back at the boy too, and she couldn't see his eyes anymore, yet by the way the boy cowered, she knew the man had shown the boy a glimpse of the monster waiting for him when the girl left.

When the man turned back to the girl, his disguise was back up as he smiled and nodded before he started inside. The girl held her breath as he walked by, afraid the monster might jump out and attack her.

But he never did.

He must save it for the boy, *she thought sadly.*

Once the monster was in his palace that looked more like a dungeon hidden beneath fancy walls, tall towers, and bright lights, she finally faced the boy.

"Are you okay?" she asked tentatively. It'd been forever since the girl had spoken to a boy—to anyone really—and she was nervous.

"I'm fine," the boy replied, the iciness in his tone startling her. Maybe she'd been wrong. Maybe the boy really couldn't see the monster living inside the man.

"O-okay." Her voice quivered as she lowered her head and turned to go back home and back though the vines that surrounded her own torturous palace.

"Wait," the boy called out before she could get too far.

The sound of his voice calmed her, and when she faced him again, she was almost smiling for the very first time in six years.

The boy kept his distance, as if he feared the girl and was afraid to get too close. But that was okay. She feared his closeness as well.

"Why did you do that?" he asked, wrapping his arms around himself.

"Because..." She considered what to tell him. The

truth? It seemed too terrifying to utter her secrets aloud. Maybe she could be vague, though. "No one ever did it for me."

"You know a monster too?" the boy asked, and this time, he took a step toward her.

The girl was afraid.

But she was also curious.

So she stayed.

"Yes," she said, "I do."

"Does he... hurt you?"

She wanted to run, but found herself nodding. "He did."

The boy seemed sad and in pain as he moved toward her again, this time more quickly and with his hand extended. "I'm sorry that he did."

The girl stared at his hand, uncertain what to do. She was afraid to touch him, afraid the boy could be wearing his own disguise and that suddenly a monster would appear in his place.

The boy must have read her mind because he pulled away and wrapped his arms around himself again. "Thank you," he uttered softly.

"For what?"

"For scaring him away."

Again, the girl almost smiled, and she could have

sworn the boy did too.

"You're welcome," she replied, then the two of them stood there in the darkness, the distant lights from the castles seeming far off, but for the first time, the light was within reach.

I end up writing until my fingers ache and my eyes and brain feel like they're bleeding. It's the most tiring and satisfying feeling ever. By the time I'm getting out of the backseat to take Jackson up to my apartment, I feel high and can't help thinking, *This is what I want forever. Just my computer, my tiny little apartment, and Kayden. I just wish I had him here with me right now.*

"So, who were you talking to on the phone the whole drive?" I ask Jackson as we trudge up the stairway. It's around noon, but the stormy sky along with the quietness of the apartment complex makes it seem like it's much later.

He shrugs, scratching at the back of his neck. "No one."

"It was your girlfriend, huh?" I tease as I take my keys out of my bag.

He gapes at me. "How'd you know?"

"Because of the way your voice sounded. All swoony." I clasp my hands together and make by best swoony impression. When Jackson actually blushes, it's so funny that I bust up laughing. "Oh, my God. I can't believe I'm just learning about her." I find the right key on the chain as we reach the door. "Do Mom and Dad know?"

"No," he swiftly says. "And I'd prefer it if you didn't say anything right now. I've just started seeing her and don't want Mom to get too attached to the idea yet, considering how she is with that stuff."

"That doesn't seem fair for me to do that, considering how much you teased me about Kayden in front of them the entire week." I stick the key in the lock and turn it, excited to be home.

"Callie, please," he begs, which he never does.

It's super funny, but I decide to be nice. "Fine, mum's the word." I push open the door and step back to let him in. "But lay off on the teasing me, okay?"

He nods as he steps inside.

"So, this is where you live?" my brother states as he circles the small living room. There's not much to look at; a small suede chair we bought at a secondhand store along with an entertainment center and a brand new television—that was the splurge. "It's a good thing Mom let you take all that shit with us, huh?"

I breathe in that fresh home scent as I shut the door behind me. "Yeah, it was really nice of her."

"I'm just trying to figure out how we're going to get all that furniture up here." Jackson glances at the window as he rubs his jawline. The window is webbed with frost and snowflakes splattered against it. "Because the tarp's not going to hold up if it keeps snowing like this, and there's no way I can carry it up here with you and your tiny arms."

I pull a face, but then let it go because he's kind of right. "It's been a really rough winter, hasn't it?" I plop down on the couch with the phone in my hand.

"I wouldn't know since I live in sunny, awesome Florida." Jackson grins conceitedly as he sits down on the armrest of the chair. "When's Kayden supposed to be here? The two of us could probably get all that shit up the stairs. I'm just super fucking relieved you're not on the third floor, although you should have picked the first floor."

"Kayden's not going to be here until Monday evening," I tell him, opening my contacts to text Luke because he's the only other strong guy I know. "And I didn't pick the floor. Or the apartment."

He raises his eyebrows at me as he stuffs his hands into the pockets of his tan cargo pants. "What do you mean?"

"I mean, Kayden picked this place out with Seth," I say with a shrug. "As a surprise for me."

"But he knew you wanted to move in with him, right?

He didn't just do it assuming that you did?" He almost seems like he's asking for knowledge for himself, like maybe he's thinking about doing it with his girlfriend.

"Of course he knew I wanted to. I'd asked him a couple of weeks before then, and he said he'd think about it, but then he surprised me with this." I gesture around at the place proudly, even though Jackson looks unimpressed. I don't care, though. This is my palace, and unlike the one in the story I'm writing, it doesn't have vines and thorns, but warmth and promises of happiness.

Then Jackson gives me a strange look that I can't decipher.

"What?" I ask.

He shrugs. "It's nothing."

"It is something, otherwise you wouldn't be looking at me like a weirdo."

That gets him to laugh. "It really is nothing. I was just thinking about how you seem happy." His shoulders keep lifting and falling. "It's nice… You deserve it."

"Thanks, Jackson." I smile at him as I text Luke to see if he can come help.

"Although, I have to say, I wouldn't tell Mom that whole story of him surprising you. She'll think you're getting engaged." He pauses then smirks at me. "Though, I wouldn't be surprised if you did at the rate you two are going."

"Okay, *Mom.*" I roll my eyes at him then laugh, but Jackson doesn't join in.

"'Just giving you a head's up," he tells me with a nonchalant lift of his shoulders. "You seem kind of clueless with this stuff."

I'd be offended, but I'm too distracted by the other thing he's said. Is that where Kayden and I are heading? Why have I never thought about this before?

I probably would have sat there all day, stuck in my thoughts, if my phone didn't start going nuts in my hand.

Luke: Yeah, headed over. I'm not at my place though, so it'll take me just a little bit longer to get there.

Me: K. Thanks. I owe u one :)

I put my phone into my pocket then rise to my feet. "I got you some non-tiny backup."

My brother looks at me like I've lost my mind. "What the hell are you talking about?"

"Luke's coming over to help you move the heavy stuff in," I say, opening the front door. "But while we wait, this tiny girl with her tiny arms is going to go bring up what she can because she's not as weak as she looks."

"I know that, Callie." My brother follows me outside

and down the stairway. "You're tougher than a lot of people."

"Wow, two compliments in a day," I joke, jumping off the last step and into a fluffy pile of snow that reaches the ankles of my boots. "It's a holiday miracle."

"It'll be a holiday miracle if it stopped snowing." He zips up his coat to his chin and glares at the cloudy sky. "I'm going to freeze my ass off."

"The weather in Florida is turning you kind of a baby." I pick up a hand full of snow and ball it up in my hand. "You know that?"

Now he's glaring at me. "If you throw that at me, you're going to pay."

I rotate the snow in my hand until it's a firm ball, then I back down the frozen sidewalk. "I'll only pay if you can catch me, but I have a feeling that Florida Boy is going to fail epically when I run up the snowbank." Then I stick out my tongue and launch the snowball at him.

I don't think he thought I had the guts to do it because he doesn't even duck. It hits him straight in the face, and I feel kind of bad, but not enough to stop myself from laughing.

Looking pissed off, he wipes the snow from his face with the sleeve of his jacket. "You're so going to pay for that." He cracks his knuckles as he ambles toward me. "I think you've forgotten how good I used to be at mad, crazy snowball fighting."

"The key words being *used to*." I take off running before I even finish my sentence, knowing full well this is probably going to end with me getting my face shoved in the snow. He used to do it all the time when we were younger, and Jackson hasn't grown up enough not to do it now.

Just like I've predicted, by the end of our mad, crazy snowball fight, Jackson is smashing snow in my face. I'm on my back on the snowbank near the dumpster, laughing my butt off as he stands over me, pressing handfuls of snow into my face. Then out of the corner of my eye, I see Luke's truck pull up and park under the carport near the building.

"Fine, I give up!" I laugh, kicking at Jackson. I feel like a kid again, having fun with my older brother, something that stopped happening when I was twelve. "Just stop! Luke's here."

"I warned you not to mess with me." His cheeks are red because I did manage to get a few more snowballs thrown at his face. Just to be an ass, Jackson drops a ball of snow on the top of my head before helping me to my feet. Then we slip down the steep hill and walk back toward the carport area. My coat is full of snow, and I try to shake it out while Jackson laughs at me.

"This is so cold," I say as we approach Luke's truck.

"Just wait until we hit the slopes," Jackson replies, plucking some snowflakes out of his hair. "You're probably going to get a face full of snow every time you try to stop."

My nose scrunches. "Way to boost my confidence."

Jackson's mouth spreads to a grin. "Any time."

I'm thinking of a comeback when the truck door swings open and Luke hops out. He's wearing a vintage leather coat, along with beanie, and he has black boots on. "

Figures it has to be snowing when we do this," Luke remarks as he slips a pair of gloves on.

Luke used to scare me when I first met him. He just has that look about him that screams back the heck off. Once I got to know him, though, I realized he is actually really nice and that the look comes from his own inner demons.

"I hope you don't mind, but I brought some people with me." Right as Luke says it, Violet climbs out of the passenger side of his truck. Like Luke, she's wearing a beanie over her wild locks of red and black hair, along with boots, and a leather jacket, only unlike Luke, Violet's jacket has studs in it. The two of them are actually a really good match and not just when it comes to looks. Although, I can seriously picture two figurine replicas of them standing upon the top of a gothic wedding cake.

"The more the merrier," Jackson tells Luke, stomping some snow off his boots. "And the less I have to carry."

"Well, aren't you just a gentlemen?" Violet inquires sarcastically, unimpressed.

My brother responds by checking her out, his eyes quickly scrolling up her body.

I jab him in the side with my elbow. "Ew, stop it," I hiss under my breath. "She's Luke's girlfriend, and you have your own, remember?"

Jackson pulls a *whoops* look, totally busted. "Sorry."

I'm surprised by how easily he lets it go.

I turn to Luke and Violet, reaching into my coat pocket to get my own gloves. "Ready to get this party started?"

"Yeah, just as soon as I bundle up." The voice doesn't come from either of them or my brother, but from someone standing near the passenger side of the truck.

My head snaps in the direction, my heart leaping in my chest before I even see him. "What the heck are you doing here?" I ask as I sprint around the back of the truck, nearly wiping out on a patch of ice. But I regain my footing and launch myself into Kayden's strong arms a little too forcefully because he lets out a grunt.

His arms enclose around me and he holds me tightly against him. "I couldn't take it anymore. I needed to be here with you."

"I needed you here, too," I say because, even though I've handled the thing with Caleb just fine, I've needed him, something I'm discovering now.

"I know." He hugs me tighter.

To everyone else, it probably looks like we're happily reuniting. That, like the apartment, this was another amazing surprise. It is in a way but only I can hear the desperation in Kayden's voice, the silent plea for me to never let him go.

And it's exactly what I do.

Chapter 22

#164 ~~Party~~ Dance Like a Rock Star.

Kayden

Dylan let me use his flyer miles to change flights and go home early, but only if I promised to visit for Christmas and bring Callie. Hopefully, Callie won't mind that I agreed because I really just wanted to go home to her.

The entire flight home, I was a mess and had to keep repeating to myself all the reasons why I didn't need to cut myself.

1. Callie.

2. I don't want to go back to that place where I become that person again.

3. I'm not happier when I do it.

4. It's unhealthy, both mentally and physically.

5. Callie.

6. I'll have to start over again.

7. My body already has too many scars.

8. I want to be better.

9. I need to let go of the past.

    10.   Callie.

    11.   Callie.

    12.   Callie.

That list streamed through my mind for the entire trip and kept me intact and clearly showed what was important to me. By the time I make it to the apartment—to Callie—I'm an emotional wreck, but in a good way.

I don't really get to talk to Callie very much for the rest of the day, even though I'm desperate to. We spend most of the afternoon unloading the truck then take a break in the living room before we head out to get something to eat because everyone is "starving to death."

"You need some pictures on your wall," Jackson comments as he takes a seat on the sofa and glances around at our bare walls. He removes the beanie he's been wearing and tosses it aside. "It'd make this place look better."

"We'll get there," Callie replies, plopping down on the barstool next to the one I'm sitting on. Luke and Violet are sprawled out on the floor, cheeks red and looking as exhausted as I feel. There are pieces of furniture and boxes everywhere, but it feels like we've made progress with turning this place into a home. "I'm still working on getting some up."

"I don't think we have any," I say, picking at the label on my water bottle. "At least, not any of you and me together."

"You don't think I've taken pictures of us?" she says, pressing her hand to her chest, feigning being offended.

I manage to peel the damp label off and set it on the counter. "You have some?"

"Of us." She nudges me with her elbow and smiles. But when I don't return it, it falters. "What's wrong?"

"It's nothing." I shrug and then lower my voice so no one else can hear me. "It's just, pictures on the wall? Is that what people do? Because my family sure as hell didn't while I was growing up." But I can't help thinking of Dylan's place and all the pictures he has up—a life, and a good one. Is that where I'm heading? Can I have that?

It's crazy that I don't have to say it, that Callie can actually knows what I'm thinking. "It'll make this place not just an apartment, but a home." She leans over and gives me a peck on the lips.

I'm about to pull her in for a deeper kiss, but Jackson clears his throat. "Okay, I say it's time to get some grub."

Callie sighs against my lips. "We'll talk later."

After I nod, we all head out and pile into Callie's dad's car, which is roomier than my car and Luke's truck. Luke still manages to turn on some classic rock that everyone pretends they don't know but ends up belting out the lyrics to. By the time we hit up a local, mellower bar in town, everyone is laughing and in a good mood yet so exhausted that it takes us forever to make it in inside.

"So much for partying like a rock star," Callie jokes to Jackson as we settle into a booth. There's some alternative music playing in the background and some people dancing. "You must be so disappointed in me."

Jackson reaches for a menu tucked between the salt shakers. "Nah, I'm kind of tired myself." He flips open the menu. "Must be getting old."

"You better watch it," she teases. "You're one step away from sitting around in your sweat pants on weekends and yelling at the television when your team fumbles the ball."

"Hey, I do that sometimes," I intervene. "Well, minus the sweatpants." I flash her a flirty grin and wink. "I just do it naked."

"Glad to know what I have to look forward to," Callie says then winks back at me. It makes me laugh for the first time since I've gotten back from Virginia.

"Good God, please don't go there," Jackson mutters with all his attention on the menu. "I really don't want to hear about what my sister and her boyfriend do behind closed doors."

"Sorry, man." I actually used to hate Jackson for the way he treated Callie and for bringing Caleb into her life. I still carry a little disdain for him, but Callie seems to have let it go, so I'm trying to be nice. I want to talk to Callie openly without her brother listening, so I move to get out of the booth and Luke gives me a begrudging huff of frustration when he has to get out of my way.

"Where are you going?" Callie asks as I stand up and stretch my arms above my head, constraining a grin when I notice her checking out the sliver of my stomach that peeks out from the bottom of my shirt.

"To dance." I nod my chin in the direction of the dance area. "Want to come?"

She shakes her head. "Nah, I kind of want to see you shaking your thing solo." When I start to frown, she laughs. "Of course I'll join you, silly boy." She's sitting between Violet and her brother and motions for Violet to let her out.

Once she's to her feet, she entwines our fingers and then we make our toward the dance floor where couples are grinding against each other.

Callie is wearing black skinny jeans tucked in lace-up boots along with a red shirt and her hair is up and the only makeup she has on is some black liner. She's probably the most dressed woman here and the most beautiful.

When we reach the center of the dance floor, I pull her close to me and she rests her head on my chest as we start swaying to the beat of "Ho Hey" by The Lumineers.

"So why'd you really come home early?" Callie utters so softly I can barely hear her over the music.

"Because I wanted to make sure you were okay." I splay my hand across her lower back, and put the other on her hips then rest my chin on the top of her head.

"But there's more to it than that." It's not a question, but a statement.

My initial reaction is to lie, but then I realize I don't want to lie to her, don't want to be that guy. "Because I wasn't handling things well."

Her arms tighten around the back of my neck. "Did you—"

"No," I cut her off so she doesn't have to ask. "I wanted to, though. Things were already hard when I learned about my father and about what happened with Caleb, but then it got worse when my mother called and wanted to talk to me."

"Did you talk to her?"

"No... I couldn't."

"Good. I'm glad. You shouldn't. Not until we know where she stands. And maybe not even then."

"I love you," I say because it's all I can say at the moment. The way she's always protecting me is too much sometimes to even comprehend.

She slants back to look me in the eyes. "I don't think you should ever even consider talking to her again unless you want to, no matter what happens."

"I won't," I assure her. "Although, I was kind of curious what she had to say… probably something bad, but still she's…"

"She's your mom, and you feel like you have to talk to her," Callie finishes for me. "But she needs to start acting like a mother before you start treating her like one."

"I'm not sure I ever want to."

"Then don't. You don't owe her anything."

Her words are exactly what I needed to hear, and I no longer want to dwell on family stuff. I want to let go of it, so I change the subject. "You and your brother seem to be getting along."

She shrugs, staring up at me with those beautiful eyes of hers. "It's been nice hanging out with him."

"Good. I'm glad. It's nice to see you happy around your family."

"My mom wants *us* to come visit," she says, emphasizing her point that I'm included in this.

"Dylan wants *us* to do the same thing," I mimic her emphasizing.

It gets her to grin, her eyes crinkling at the corners. "Families are needy, aren't they?" As soon as she says it, she looks worried, like she's offended me or something.

"Callie, you don't have to be careful with me. You can say the word family, and I'll be fine." I catch her gaze flick to my wrist, which I'm proud to say is free of any fresh cuts. "And besides, I'm learning that family doesn't always mean what I thought it did. Dylan and his wife are nice, and Tyler wasn't a dick when I got to see him" Keeping one hand on Callie's back, I place the other gently on her cheek. "But honestly, you're more of my family than any-one else. All I need is you and me and our apartment, and I'm good. I realized that while I was in Virginia."

She swallows hard, her eyes watering up, but she looks happy, not sad. "Good, because it's all I need, too." Then she stands up on her tiptoes and plants a soft kiss on my mouth. "From now on," she whispers against my lips, "we take all trips and vacations together."

"Deal," I say then coax her lips apart with my tongue to kiss her as deeply as I've been wanting to all day.

We keep moving and kissing until the song ends. When it switches to a faster tempo one, I decide to step up my skills. Like the first time we danced, I slide my hand down Callie's arm, push her out then spin her around until she crashes into my chest.

She throws her head back and busts up laughing. "You know, we may not have gotten to party like rock stars, but we sure as heck can dance like them."

"We sure as hell can," I say, spinning her around and around until she's laughing so hard she's crying. "We can do anything—you and I—when we're together."

Her laughing silences as she stares up at me. "I want this... you and I... forever."

I wet my lips with my tongue, noting how much my heart accelerates, noticing how much I don't want to run.

Stay.

Stay.

Stay.

My heart beats.

Forever.

And ever.

And ever.

"Me, too," I say then kiss her with as much passion as my heart is carrying, letting her know just how much I love her, and that I always will.

Chapter 23
#165 Accept the Phone Call You've Been Dreading.

Kayden

A week passes without anything major happening, and I start think that maybe my life may finally be getting some normalcy. My days consist of practice, school, Callie, work, Callie, and practice. I love the routine, and it gets me wondering if maybe Dylan was right, perhaps it's time to let everything go with my father. Move on. Accept that football might be my thing and simply own it. It doesn't need to be associated with my father if *I* don't want it to be.

Yep, everything is going great in that thing we call life until I got that goddamn call.

The thing is, I knew it was coming, knew it would happen eventually. But what I wasn't prepared for was who would deliver the news to me. Maybe if I did, I could have prepared myself more.

The unknown number should have been a red flag, but I was working on a final paper for class and was distracted when I answered it.

God, I wish I wouldn't have been distracted.

"Your father's dead." The sound of my mother's voice sidetracks me from what she's said.

"How the fuck did you get my number?" I shove the textbooks off the bed and sit up. "Did Dylan give it to you?" If so, then I'm super pissed. And hurt.

She laughs hollowly, sounding like the unemotional zombie she always when I was growing up. "Yeah, right. Like he would ever do that. He thinks he's protecting you from us by keeping us disconnected."

I'm relieved Dylan didn't betray me. And I'm a little pissed off at myself for instantly jumping to that conclusion. "He is, though. Protecting me."

"Well, you can believe what you want," she snaps, her icy tone unsettlingly familiar. "But people shouldn't disown their family."

"I didn't disown you. You chose to leave, and I chose not to let you back in to my life." I swing my legs over the edge of the bed and put my feet on the floor. "And I've been doing fine with that choice—better than I have my entire life."

"Well, I'm sorry we make you so miserable." She sounds anything other than sorry. Irritated, yes. Sorry, no. There's a pause and I think she's waiting for me to disagree with her statement, but I'm not going to. "Well, anyway. I thought I'd call to let you know you're now officially fatherless."

"Okay." Again, I feel nothing.

Nothing.

Empty.

Cold.

Without a heart.

Except I do have a heart.

It just beats for someone else.

People who deserve its beat.

Callie.

"Jesus, Kayden, you could at least pretend to sound upset about it," she says in a surprisingly even tone for someone who just lost her husband.

"Yeah, well, I guess I'm not as good at pretending as you are." I lower my head into my hand, wanting to retract what I just said because it's rude and spiteful, and I don't want to be that kind of person. But I can't bring myself to *pretend.*

"I can't believe how you're acting," she snaps. "I raised you to be better than this. I raised you to be the kind of person that would at least come say good-bye to their father before he passed. You know how weird it looked to the doctors and nurses when none of his children showed up?" My mother has always been into appearances, her motto being, "as long as everyone thinks everything is perfect, then it is."

"About as bad as it looked for the entire town when I got arrested, I'm sure. Or when I was committed because of my cutting."

"I can't believe you're bringing that up."

"And I can't believe you called me." I get up from the bed and start pacing the room, trying to channel my adrenaline in the healthiest way I can think of. *I will not give in. I won't.* "Dylan could have given me the update."

"Update? I can't believe you just called your father's death an update." She's verging toward crying. I should feel bad, but I can't find the will to bring that emotion out of me for her. "After everything he did for you. Put you into sports. Put a roof over your head. Bought you all the things you needed."

"There's so much more to life than materialism, Mother. And so much more to being a parent than buying your children the shit they need, like say, loving them and not beating them up or stabbing them."

"I didn't do any of those things." She tries to sound calm, but I can tell she's crying and nearing toward completely losing it, which is something I've never seen or heard her do before.

I should stop.

I should care enough to stop.

But I don't.

"No, you just let it happen," I say through gritted teeth, "which is just as bad."

"We are not bad parents!" she cries hysterically, shocking me—I honestly didn't think she possessed emotion. "We're not..." The last sounds like she's trying to convince herself, not me.

I can't take it anymore. Bad mother or not, I don't want to be the kind of person to bring others pain. Don't want to be like them. Don't want to carry this heaviness in me anymore. I want to let it go—be free. So I make a choice, one that will hopefully set me free.

"I'm sorry."

"For what?"

"For saying all those things..." *Even though they're true.*

"Good. Now, let's talk about your father's funeral and what you can help me with."

I stop pacing. "No."

"What?" She sounds shocked.

"I'm not helping you with any of that."

"But he's your father..." It's sad that that's the best argument she can come up with. "And you just said you were sorry."

"Yeah, for saying hateful things." I breathe through the pain tearing at my chest, through the tears starting to emerge. I'm letting go—accepting what is. I can feel myself on the verge of it. But the thing is, I'm letting go of a lot, and I'm worried I'm going to explode when I finally say good-bye to it all—the hate, the pain, the resentment. "But not for feeling the way that I do. I'll never be sorry for that, nor will I help with his funeral."

"So you're not coming?" She's still crying, but she sounds infuriated.

"I might, but I'm not sure yet." I grab my car keys and jacket before heading out of the room. "You can give Dylan the details, and then he can pass them along to me."

"You're a terrible son."

The only things that stop me from listing all the terrible things she is is: 1) She's hurting, and even though I despise her, I don't want to be that person. And 2) It doesn't matter; she's my past if I choose to let her be.

And I think I do.

"That's your opinion"—I jerk open the front door, telling myself to continue breathing, to continue doing what I'm doing. Moving forward... move forward... one step at a time—"and I can live with that." I make another choice and hang up, not giving her any more room to insult me or make me angry.

Then I head for my car and in the direction of quite possibly the best choice I have ever made.

Chapter 24

#166 Hold Someone While They Let it All Out.

Callie

Not too much has happened since Thanksgiving holiday. Kayden and I finished up the break by going snowboarding Jackson. Then we spent some time together—finally—in our new home.

I went and visited Harper a couple of times to make sure everything was going okay with therapy. She seemed less fake and a bit more real, so when she told me things are going well, I believed her. It makes me happy that I've been able to help her with that, almost as if it was a healing process for me as well, one I wasn't aware I needed.

School goes on. Football goes on. Writing goes on. Life goes on. The next week goes by pretty uneventfully. But the thing that Kayden and I both knew was coming finally arrives, smack dab in the middle of finals. I'm actually finishing up a test in Oceanography when I get a call from Kayden. I only know it's him because of the ringtone, but I can't answer it if I don't want to get accused of cheating.

I hurry and finish up the last of the questions then grab my bag and rush out of the classroom, tossing the exam on the teacher's desk as I go by. As soon as I'm out into the fairly empty hallway, I dig my phone out of my pocket and call Kayden back.

"Hey, what's up?" I ask when he answers.

He takes a deep breath, and immediately, I know whatever he's called for has to be bad. "It's my dad. He's dead."

My heart slams against my chest. "I'll be right there." I practically run for the exit doors at the end of the hallway. All I can picture is Kayden locked in the bathroom with a razor in his hand. "Are you at home?"

"No, I'm actually in the parking lot." Emotion surfaces through his voice and crack through the reception between us, and I swear I can actually feel everything he's feeling. "I needed to see you, so I've been sitting out here, waiting for you to get out of class."

"I'm coming." I burst out the doors and sprint across the snowy campus yard, grasping onto the handle of bag. "Where are you parked?"

"At the front." Vulnerability edges through his voice, like he's fighting not to break apart before I get there.

I scan the parking lot, and when I spot his car, I veer right, not slowing down until I'm in the car and I shut the door, locking out the outside world. Then I turn to Kayden who is sitting in the driver's seat, staring ahead at the campus quad with his jaw set tight as his chest rises and crashes. He has on his pajama pants and a hoodie, which means he probably left the house in a hurry. The silence chills my heart. I'm uncertain what to say—if there's anything I can. What the heck does one say to someone in this type of situation?

I'm sorry.

That you lost your dad.

Lost the monster in your life.

That you're hurting.

That you're confused.

That you have to go through this.

"I love you." It's all I can think of, and it seems to be exactly what he needs to hear because he rotates toward to me, his eyes watering over as he leans over and wraps his arms around me, crashing against me. My stomach presses into the console, but I still surrender into his arms as he hugs me almost in desperation.

"I love you, too," he whispers with his head buried in my neck. "God, I fucking love you. And, really, that's all that matters." I can feel the exact moment when he starts to sob, not because I feel his tears or even hear him. I feel it because of how tight his hold gets on me, like every one of his muscles has to ravel in order to force the emotion out of him.

I enfold my arms around him and run my fingers through his hair, remaining quiet while he cries because there's not much more I can do. He needs to get it out, and I'm glad he is. It's when he keeps things in that it becomes a problem.

I'm not even sure how long we sit there like that, well into the evening, but I don't dare move, afraid he'll suck all the emotion back inside himself and trap it in.

By the time he moves away, the sky has cleared, but the sun is lowering behind the mountains, casting an orange and neon glow against the snow on the ground. There are hardly any people left on campus and the parking lot is nearly vacant.

"Are you okay?" I ask as he wipes his bloodshot eyes with the back of his hand.

"Yeah, sorry about that." His voice is hoarse "I just lost it for a second."

"You know, it's okay to lose it." I reach over to wipe away a few remaining tears on his face. I'm about to pull my hand back when he leans into my touch, so I keep my palm on his cheek. "And it's okay to cry."

"I know it is," he says, letting out an exhale. "And I

think I needed to do it—let it all out. I've needed to for the last twenty years."

He pauses and I'm about to ask if he wants to talk about it when he leans back in the seat, faces forward, and puts the car into reverse. "I know you have questions," he says as I buckle my seatbelt. "And I'll answer them, but I just want to be home when I do, if that's okay?"

I nod, turning forward in my own seat. "Of course that's okay."

He looks relieved as he drives out of the parking lot and onto the street. On our way back to the apartment, we stop to pick up some takeout because neither one of us are great—nor do we enjoy—cooking. Then we settle on the sofa with our hamburgers, fries, and drinks and eat in silence, even though it just about drives me crazy.

"It was my mother who called," he finally says as he picks up his drink and fiddles with his straw. "She found out my number and called to tell me herself."

"Was she…?" I pick at my hamburger. "Was she nice?"

He shakes his head as he takes a sip of his drink. "No, she was exactly herself."

Okay, now I'm really worried. "Kayden, I—"

He cuts me off by leaning forward and brushing his

lips across mine. When he pulls away, he seems content. "I'm fine, Callie. I promise." As if to prove this point, he sets his food down on the coffee table and takes my hand in his. "I got to tell her a lot of stuff I never had the balls to, and then I realized that I was done."

"Done?"

"With all of it. With her. With hating both of them. With letting them still affect my life even when they're not in it anymore." He takes my burger from my hand, sets it down by his, and scoots toward me until our knees touch. "I'm going to let it go." Determination pours from his eyes and overpowers me to the point I feel like I'm drowning in the pain he's releasing himself from. "I'm going to focus on the future, keep going to school, and play my fucking heart out and hope I get drafted. And if I don't, I'll have my degree to fall back on." He tucks strands of hair behind my ear, before spreading his warm fingers across my cheek. "And I'm going to take care of you and make you so happy." Emotion radiates through his gaze as he steadily holds mine. "I want to keep going down this path with you. I want us to have a future—you and me."

Maybe Jackson was right. Maybe we are headed in the direction of marriage. God, what if we are? Do I want it?

I nod eagerly. "I want that too, more than anything else... But..."

His forehead creases, his confidence descending. "But what?"

"But..." I hesitate, nervous to bring it up. "But what about the funeral? Are you...? Are you going to go to it?"

"I'm not sure yet." He's not angry or sad, just confused.

"Well, either way, I support you." I turn my head and delicately kiss his palm. "I'm here for you if you want to go and say good-bye. Get some closure, maybe."

His expression is full of nothing except love. "I know you're here for me." It's within that moment I realize that we're going to be okay. Sure, there will probably be bumps down the road for us—there always will be when it comes to life—but he's finally letting me love him like he deserves, and that's a huge, epic step for us.

Life changing, even.

The rest of the night is relaxing, falling into our routine. We eat. We talk. Then after Kayden falls asleep in bed, I write.

I'm starting to love our routine.

As soon as my fingers hit the keys, they come alive, eager to write and be free.

After the girl saved the boy, they didn't see each other for many sun rises and sun sets. Not because they chose to,

236

but because they'd gone their separate ways and done their separate things, which is the case most times in life.

The girl had moved out of her palace and found a new place to live—a new life for herself where she wasn't constantly haunted by the memories of the monster. She actually felt happier than she had in a long time, partly because she'd been able to leave her past behind, but also because the night she had saved the boy, something had changed inside her. She'd stood up to a monster, and although it wasn't her own, it had made her feel braver and less fearful in a world that seemed so scary all the time.

And the boy... Well, she didn't know what had become of the boy, if he'd escaped the monster or not, but she hoped so. Hoped he was moving on like her.

Hoped he'd found happiness in those sad eyes of his.

It was during a warm, fall day that she found out what he'd been doing. Their reuniting was anything other than magical, but it was still momentous, a literal crashing into each other when they just happened to be in the same place at the same time.

Smack.

They ran into each other head on, the impact intense, but not as much as seeing each other again.

They were in shock.

Stunned.

Breathless.

But most of all, they were simply glad to see each other alive and breathing.

"Hey," the girl said as the wind and leaves danced around them.

"Hey," the boy replied back, looking better than he had before. His eyes, although they still carried sadness, also carried happiness.

Their first words weren't the best of opening liners, not like in the fairytales the girl had read back when she was a princess. Stories that promised fantasies of princes sweeping a princess off their feet, wooing hearts with words and sometimes songs.

But that was okay.

She didn't need wooing.

She didn't need songs.

Because she wasn't a princess.

And the boy wasn't a prince.

She was just a girl.

And he was just a guy.

And this wasn't a fairytale.

But real life.

And fairytales were overrated anyway.

The rest of their conversation was light, cautious, nei-

ther of them comfortable enough to bring up that night. They soon parted ways with a wave and a smile that carried hope that they would soon see each other again.

It was not the end for these two.

There was so much more in store for them.

Now that their monsters were out of their lives.

It didn't start right away—the relationship between the two of them. They had a class together and their conversations were filled with, "Can I borrow a pen?" and "Did you go to my game on Friday?" and "You should really go to my game."

The girl wanted to say more and so did the guy, but it took some time to work up the courage to take that extra step.

But, finally, that time arrived.

"So I was thinking," the guy said one day when they'd run into each other in the hallway. He was standing up straighter these days, more confident now that he wasn't being beaten down. "That we should go out some time."

"Like on a date?" The girl had never been out on a date and was confused. Yes, they'd talked a little bit to one another and she couldn't stop thinking about him—her journal was filled with pages of their average encounters, and of course, the details of his eyes because those were her favorite part—but other than that, they seemed like they

239

were going to be friends, which was way better than not being friends. Yet now, his expression showed signs of something else, as if he'd been trying to fight it but gave it up and let it free.

I like you, *his expression conveyed.*

I like you, too, *the girl wanted to say.*

"Yeah, on a date." He seemed amused by the girl and almost nonchalant about the whole thing, but his eyes promised.

I like you a lot.

I like you a lot, too.

"Okay." It was hard for the girl to say it, and when the words left her lips, they surprised her.

They surprised the guy, too, as if he'd thought she was going to say no. If she didn't know any better, she would have sworn they both stood a little taller.

"Okay, then," the guy replied. "I'll pick you up to-night."

"Okay."

Then they parted ways, the girl's head swimming with possibilities.

But could she trust him?

Because, in a world full of monsters, it was hard to tell who was what.

Chapter 25
#167 Say Good-bye.

Kayden

It's not until Dylan calls me the next day that I decide to go to the funeral because he says he's going to go. Tyler's not going though, because he's worried it might send him back into a relapse, which I understand. I honestly keep waiting for something to set me off and do the same thing, but I feel strangely okay.

I think Callie's relieved when I tell her I'm going to the funeral, like she thinks it will give me a sense of closure. I'm not sure if she's right, but it's the only chance I'm going to get, so I take it.

The funeral is in North Carolina where I just found out my mother grew up, which is why my father and her had been hiding out there—because they knew people. Callie comes with me, thankfully, but we can only stay for two days because finals are going on, and there's no way I'm going to mess up my grades or hers for this. With the limited time we have there, we mostly just hang out on the beach near our hotel.

And I'm okay with that.

In fact, it's perfect.

"I'm starting to become a fan of the ocean," Callie states the morning of the funeral. She's sitting between my legs in the sand, leaning against my chest, the sun beaming down on us. "It's so peaceful."

I'm playing with her hair as the ocean crashes against the shore just a few feet in front of us. "Yeah it is."

She nuzzles closer to me and lets out a content sigh. "We should come here more often." She adjusts her sunglasses over her eyes. "Well, not to North Carolina, but to the ocean."

"We could always live by the ocean," I say, putting one arm around her and leaving the other in the sand to support our weight, "after we graduate. Maybe I'll get lucky and get drafted to a team that's nearby the coast."

"I love hearing you talking about your future." She turns her head and looks at me. "It always worried me when you wouldn't."

I lift her sunglasses away from her face so I can her eyes. "I'm sorry it took me so long to get to that point, but I'm glad you waited for me."

"You're worth the wait," she says, breathing in deeply.

Then she starts grinning and shaking her head at herself. "You've also turned me into a walking romance novel, FYI."

"I'm not sure I know what you mean…"

She leans back to look at me "I keep uttering these cheesy lines every time I'm around you. It's becoming ridiculous."

I chuckle softly. "I think it's cute."

"Well, you do it too," she says, amused. "All the time."

I start to scrunch up my nose and protest, but then I realize she's right. So instead, I get to my feet, brush the sand off my hands, pick her up, and throw her over my shoulder.

"Kayden, what the heck!" she cries out through her laughter as she pounds on my back. I rush toward the water and wade in until I'm waist deep. We're not in shorts or swimsuits, and the water is lukewarm yet still not comfortable, but it's fun.

"This is for turning me into a sap," I tease, pinching her ass before I lower her into the water with a splash.

She lets out a squeal as the salty ocean seeps through her clothes all the way up to just below her chest. "You are a mean, mean boy."

"No way. I'm a sappy guy, thanks to you." I give her a lopsided grin as I grab the front of her shirt and haul her closer to me. Her hair is dripping wet, water droplets covering her skin, and her clothes cling to her body. She's ridiculously sexy, and I simply want to lick the water right off her skin.

So I do.

Dipping my head toward her neck, I lick a path across her collarbone, ignoring the salty taste.

"Kayden," she gasps, her fingers tangling through my damp hair.

When she pulls me closer, I smile against her skin as I drop my head lower and my hands glide up to her stomach. I kiss a path to the collar of her shirt then pull it down to suck on the curve of her breast. She struggles to stand upright against the intensity and the waves rolling toward us, so I reach down, grab her thigh, and hitch it around my hip. She gasps and rolls her hips against me. The moment is perfect, and I'm about to give our bodies everything they're craving when a large wave comes slamming against us and knocks us apart.

"Holy shit." I struggle to get my footing as Callie comes up from out of the water.

"Serves you right"—she laughs and swims toward shore—"for throwing me in there to begin with," she coughs as she crawls out of the water and drops down on the sand, exhausted.

I wade out and lie down beside her, completely unconcerned that the sand is getting caked to my clothes. Then we stare at the sky, getting lost in the peace of just being near each other. But it's when the clouds roll in that I'm reminded of why we're here.

"We should probably get ready to go," Callie whispers with her arm draped over her forehead.

I slowly nod. "Yeah, you're probably right." It takes us a minute to move, and in the end, I wish we could have stayed.

Just her and I.

Callie and me.

The warm sand.

The peaceful ocean.

That's all I want.

Yet, deep down, I know it's time for me to go say good-bye.

Dylan and Liz show up to pick us up from our hotel a few hours before the funeral to take us out for lunch. Callie's wearing a black dress that looks a lot like Liz's, and Dylan and I are wearing black pants, white shirts, and black ties that look similar. None of our moods seem as sullen as our outfits, though.

245

"I can't believe you're a writer," Liz says to Callie from across the table at the fast food place we're eating at. "That's so cool."

Callie seems a little self-conscious with the attention focused solely on her. "Yeah, I guess, but I still have a lot of stuff to do if I'm going to make writing my career."

I drape my arm around her and comb my fingers through her hair that still has the faintest scent of ocean in it. "You *are* going to be one. It's what you love to do."

She scrunches up her face. "I just don't want to think of it as a job, you know. The internship is great and everything, but I don't know. It's just not as fun as writing stories."

"You should write stories, then. If that's what you want to do," I say, picking up a fry and popping it into my mouth.

"Easier said than done." She dunks a fry into a cup of ranch. "Do you know how hard of a career that is to get into?"

"You can do it," I say with a smile. "And I'll take care of you while you do." *I promise I'll take care of you,* I mouth.

"You guys are adorable," Liz interrupts our little moment. When I look across the table, I realize they're both watching us with fascination. "Seriously, like the cutest thing I've ever seen."

Dylan rolls his eyes. "Don't worry. She thinks everything's adorable. Puppies, kittens, bedding, cars, movies, old people." He flashes her a grin.

"Oh, whatever," she says, teasingly swatting him in the chest. "You get all misty-eyed during movies, too."

As he keeps grinning at her, she throws a fry at his face, but he opens his mouth and catches it. We're all having fun, and I almost forget why we're here until Liz gets up from the booth.

"It's time to go," she tells everyone with a sigh as she glances at the clock on the wall.

This somber silence sets over us as we're forced back to reality and the real reason the four of us our here, hanging out in North Carolina.

To say good-bye.

"I guess it is," Dylan mutters as he gets up and starts for the door, fumbling to get the car keys from his pocket.

We all follow in silence and get into the car. The drive to the church doesn't seem long enough. I wish I could make it last forever. We ride in my brother's rental car, Callie and I sitting in the backseat and holding hands the entire way, which helps me breathe easier. The air is humid, the ocean is the scenery for most of the way. It's calming, but I still feel my heart thumping deafeningly inside my chest the closer we get to the place.

This is it.

Can I handle it?

Finally, we arrive at a small, almost rundown looking church, which is located on the same street as the cemetery. The parking lot has hardly any cars in it, which makes me wonder if we're at the right place. But I don't say anything since Dylan seems positive this is where the funeral is at because "this is where the GPS took us."

When we're walking up the sidewalk to the church, Dylan suddenly grabs my arm and pulls me back, motioning at Callie and Liz to go ahead. Liz and Callie give us both a strange look as they pause in front of the large doors.

"It's okay," Dylan tells Liz at the same time I say, "I'm fine."

With reluctance, they both go inside, leaving Dylan and I standing at the bottom of the stairs in the shadows of the trees.

"So, if things start to get too heavy in there, just say so and we'll go," he says, fiddling around with the watch on his wrist. He seems as uneasy as I feel.

"Okay." I glance at the door and then back to him, realizing that once I go inside, things are going to change. A chapter in my life is going to be closed, and however I feel about it, in the end, I'm saying good-bye forever, like when Dylan left the house at eighteen. "I have a question, though... about how dad died..." I have no clue why I'm asking other than it seems like I should know before I walk in there, before I say good-bye and close the chapter. "Do you know what exactly happened that put him in the hospital?"

Dylan appears uneasy, loosening his tie. "I do, but are you sure you want to hear it?"

It takes me a beat to answer, but in the end, it feels like I should know. "Yeah, I think I need to, for closure."

He sighs then rakes his hand through his hair, staring out at the parking lot. "I don't know all the details, but it was a fight."

Shock ripples through me and slams against my chest. "What?"

Dylan sighs, his gaze landing back on me. "He finally got into a fight with someone who fought back." He shakes his head and then stares at one of large oak trees that are around the churchyard. "It's kind of tragic when you think about it. So much useless and unnecessary rage for all those years finally led him to the end. It was such a waste, to live life like that."

"I know it was," I utter quietly. "Being happy is so

much better, isn't it?"

Nodding, Dylan looks at me again, and the edginess in his eyes has vanished, only pity remains. Not for me, but I think for our dad. "It really, really is. Too bad he could never figure that out."

Silence wraps around us, and even though we don't agree that it's time to go in, we both move for the door at the same time and enter the church. It's about as empty as the parking lot with a few people sitting on the benches, faces I don't recognize except for one person who I knew would be there and who I was dreading seeing.

My mother.

She's sitting at the front, dressed in black with a hat on her head and a veil over her face. She turns her head when we enter, the hinges of the church door announcing our presence. We exchange a look that I don't know the meaning of, nor do I care to find out. When she starts to get up, I rip my gaze away from her and take a seat beside Callie because that's where I belong. I'm surprised when my mother takes the hint and sits back down in the bench, staring ahead at the coffin up front. It looks incredibly lonely up there with no flowers around it, no large photo to represent the man that he was.

Callie holds my hand the entire time. We don't say

much, but there's not much to say. Besides, she's here with me, and that's all that really matters—that she loves me enough to be here for me.

As the funeral goes on, the emptier the church feels with the lack of crying. There's no heart-warming eulogy dedicated to him. No one has anything to say.

There is only silence.

Emptiness.

Which is really what his life was, wasn't it?

It's in that moment, I feel sort of sorry for my dad. What a waste, to live life with so much anger that there's no room for love. I'm grateful I'm not like him. Grateful I have the chance to move on from all the pain and hate he inflicted in my life. Grateful I'm capable of love. Grateful for Callie, my brother, Liz, Luke, Violet, Seth, Greyson, and even my coach. Because, in the end, I've realized I'm not my father.

I'm simply me.

And that's enough.

I wish I could say that toward the end of his funeral, when we take him to the cemetery to put him in his finally resting place, I find it in my heart to say a few words that meant something.

But I can't.

All I can say is good-bye.

And let the past go.

Forever.

Chapter 26

#168 Try Not to Get Too Embarrassed in the Most Embarrassing Situation.

Callie

Ever since the funeral, Kayden seems to be doing a lot better. I don't ask him why because it doesn't really matter. All that does matter is the darkness that has always haunted him seems to have lifted. Don't get me wrong, he's not happy all the time, but no one ever is.

It's Christmas day, which we're spending at my parents' house. We've been there for a few days now and plan to stay through New Year's. I had suggested we go to Virginia, not only because I know that Kayden's brother wanted us to come out there, but because I knew my mother was going to act like a weirdo. Plus, there was the fact that I was worried I'd run into Caleb again, though my mother assured me he is behind bars, awaiting his trial for drug charges. But Kayden wanted to go to my home. He said it was fair that we came here since I'd already spent time with his brother and sister-in-law. I didn't feel too good about it since the time I spent with his brother and sister-in-law were at the funeral, but he promised me he really wanted to go visit my family.

Poor guy didn't know what he was in store for.

"I love Christmas," my mother singsongs as she waltzes around, picking up pieces of wrapping paper and putting them in a large garbage bag. She has on green sweater, tan pants, and her socks have Christmas trees on them, and she's dancing to Christmas music playing from the antique record player in the corner of the room. "It's the best time of the year."

"You say that about Halloween and Thanksgiving, too," I say, glancing at Kayden who has a fist balled in front of his mouth to hide his chuckling at my mother's madness. It's so embarrassing, but I'm trying my hardest not to get embarrassed because I need to get used to it—Kayden learning all my family's little quirks.

"And Valentine's Day and the Fourth of July," my dad adds as he stacks the presents we just opened beside the Christmas tree. He has on a red and green sweatshirt my mother has made him wear all day to celebrate the festivities. "Not to mention New Year's."

"Oh, I have so many plans for New Year's." My mother sets the trash bag down and walks over to me, beaming.

"I was thinking you and I could go shopping, get our hair done, then we could all go out to dinner." She glances at Kayden before looking at me. "All four of us."

I open my mouth to say… Well, something that will get us out of that mess, but my father chimes in, giving me a devious look. "Actually, sweetie," he says to my mother. "I had something really special planned for you and I."

"Really?" She claps her hands together and rushes over to him to give him a big hug.

Run, my dad mouths from over my mother's shoulder with a grin. *Run while you can.*

He doesn't have to ask me twice. I snatch ahold of Kayden's hand and yank him out of the living room.

"Oh, my God," I mutter, guiding Kayden by the sleeve of his shirt across the kitchen and toward the back door and away from my mother. Once we're out of the house, I pick up the pace, hurrying across the driveway to the garage, worried my mother's going to follow us. "I seriously think she's like one step away from locking us in the house so she can keep us forever."

Kayden chuckles, amused by my embarrassment as he pinches my cheeks, like my mom has done to me a thousand times. "What can I say? I'm super lovable enough to want to keep me forever." He's quoting something my mother said to him earlier when we were opening presents.

"You are lovable," I tell him once we get inside the guestroom that's above the garage and the door is safely shut behind us. And locked. "But she doesn't need to tell you that every minute." I flop down onto the air mattress, which is the only piece of furniture besides the space heater. I'm not complaining, though, since the reason it's so bare is because the furniture now fills our apartment.

"She's just being nice," Kayden says, gazing down at me. His hair is ruffled, his jawline scruffy, and he looks completely happy. "And it's good that she wants to be so nice. It could be worse than an overnice mother."

"Yeah, I know," I sigh, knowing he's right, that it could be worse, that I could have parents like his mother. "I just wish she'd be just a little bit less embarrassing." I raise my hand and make a pinching gesture with my fingers. "Maybe just a teeny, tiny bit."

"Yeah, I doubt that's ever going to happen." Kayden slips off his shirt and chucks it aside. His jeans ride low on his hips, giving me a view of his defined abs and chest that are crisscrossed with scars. "I did find it funny when she kept cracking jokes about us getting married all through dinner." He kneels down on the mattress, nudging my knees open with his until I spread my legs open.

"Oh, God." Shaking my head, I cover my face with my

hands. "I'm glad you find it funny because I'm sure most guys would be running for their lives."

The mattress shifts as he leans over me and places a hand on each side of my head. I crack my fingers apart and look at him. He's been so much happier since the funeral, after he said good-bye to his mother and put the past behind him. He seems to breathe freer, smile more often, and it's probably one of the most beautiful sights I've ever seen.

"Well, just make sure you really want this," I say as he pulls one of my hands away from my eyes, "because you still have time to run."

He shakes his head. "No running here," he whispers in a raspy voice I know only means one thing—he wants me. "Ever." He moves my other hand away from my face then pins my arms above my head.

A while ago, the movement would have sent my heart soaring and not in a good way. But now… Well, it freaking soars like a bird high up in the sky, never wanting to return to land. It soars because it's free.

It soars for him.

"You want me," I tease as he leans down to kiss me.

"You're right," he says. "And then I want to give you your present."

"But you already gave me my present." I pat my pocket where the tickets to the concert are that he gave me this morning. He said it's for a redo of a night that should have been special, but he couldn't give it to me then. That he's ready now to give me everything I deserve—his words not mine. My mom practically fainted when he said it. And me… Well, I think I fell in love with Kayden even more.

"Yeah, but that present was only the first part." He kisses me then, softly biting my bottom lip before leaning back for air. "There's more," he breathes against my lips, coming in for another kiss, "but you have to wait."

"Until when?" I ask, breathless, my heart skipping a beat as his hands travel to the button of my jeans.

"Until we're done with this." He gives me a wicked grin as he flicks my button undone.

"That feels like blackmail…" My back arches as his knuckles graze the bottom of my stomach. "It's a good thing I like being blackmailed by you."

"God, I love that look in your eyes when I touch you," he murmurs against my ear before softly grazing his teeth across my lobe.

I'm about to get lost inside him when I remember something. "Wait." I put a hand against his chest, pushing him back a little and causing him to give a sexy, frustrated growl that makes the area between my thighs tingle. "Don't you want your present?"

258

He pushes back from me with his brow arched. "I thought that sweater was from all of you." He's totally amused with himself.

I scowl at him. "You did not. I would never, ever be a part of giving you a sweater with an elf knitted on it."

"Hey, I like the sweater," he insists, actually being genuine. "No one has ever given me a sweater. Fuck, no one has ever given me a present before."

Wow, I can feel the pressure. Maybe I should have gotten something better than what I did.

"Well, don't get too excited," I say, scooting out from under him and rolling off the mattress. "It's not much." I reach into my duffel bag to get his present.

He sits up on the mattress, looking about as eager as a kid sitting in front of a Christmas tree. "I'll be happy with whatever you give me."

I know he's telling the truth, but still, when I hand him the small, rectangular present, I feel like it's not enough.

I hold my breath in anticipation as I take a seat beside him and he tears the paper off and chucks it aside. I wait for his reaction, but he just sits there, frozen, staring at what I gave him.

He stares.

And stares.

And stares.

With his head tucked down, I can't read him at all.

"I told you I took pictures of us." I tap the frame that's around the picture of Kayden and me kissing at the carnival we went to this summer. It's actually a really pretty picture, the flashing neon lights and shapes of the rides behind us contrasting perfectly with the starry sky above us. "Well, Seth actually took this one with my phone, but it's a gorgeous photo of us. Totally wall worthy, I think."

When he just keeps staring at the photo, I feel like I'm about to lose my mind as I think of all the things that could be wrong. Maybe I'm reminding him of his past too much. Maybe I'm reminding him of everything he didn't have.

But when I finally work up the courage to say something, a tear slips from his eye.

He's crying, and I'm afraid.

Maybe this was too emotional.

Maybe it was the wrong thing.

As my self-doubts wash over me, he lifts his gaze to meet mine, and I realize that I was wrong.

He's not crying because he's sad.

He's crying because he feels loved.

And, good God, do I love him. More than anything else in the world.

He never does say anything. He only attacks me, his

lips crashing into mine and stealing the breath right out of my lungs. But that's okay; I'll give him my air, my heart, my soul, whatever he wants. The only thing that matters is that he wants it.

"Do you remember the last time we were in this room?" he asks through his panting when we finally come up for air.

I nod, gazing up at his swollen lips before allowing my eyes to reside on his. "I do. It was the first time we made love."

"And it was one of the most amazing moments of my life," he says, his body heat warming every inch of me. "Did you know that?" he asks. When I shake my head, he whispers, "Well, it was. And even though I didn't know it at the time, it was the moment I fell in love with you."

His words sink through my skin and shoot straight to my heart. "I think it was when I fell in love with you, too," I whisper.

There's a pause, a silent exchange that words can't express.

Then we start ripping off each other's clothes. Buttons fly. Fabric gets thrown. We're laughing and smiling, and he's crying and so am I for reasons I can't even understand. It's like I'm feeling everything all at once, and it's so overwhelming and powerful. I wouldn't trade it for anything in the world.

When he slips inside me with his body over mine, all I can think about is how safe I feel in a place that once felt like it was surrounded by thorns and vines. A place that felt wholly unsafe. A place where I lost it all, but now I'm being given it all back and more.

No, Kayden is not my prince, nor have I become a princess again.

I am simply Callie.

And he is simply Kayden.

And we are simply us.

And it's the realest form of perfection that's ever existed.

"What are you doing?" Kayden asks as I sit up from the mattress and stretch my hands over my head. It's late, well past midnight, and I've been lying there for what feels like hours, trying to fall asleep, but it's not working for me. My brain is on—and I mean *on*—with words and sentences begging to be written.

"Nothing." I reach for his shirt and slip it over my head. "I was just going to do a little writing because I can't sleep."

He rolls to his side and props up on his elbow as I hurry for my bag to get my laptop. "So when do I get to read this mystery story?" he asks.

I consider what he's said as I run back to the mattress, rushing because the bare floor is freezing my feet. "When it's finished."

He glances from the laptop to me then cocks his brow. "And when will that be?"

I recline against the wall and position the laptop on my lap. "Probably tonight. I can feel the ending nearing." I open the computer and click on the screen. "Or at least the open-ended one."

"What's it about?" He leans over and reads the title on the screen. "The Truthful Fairytale... It sounds like it's about a princess and a prince."

I shake my head as I put a pillow behind my back and stretch out my legs. "Nope. Just a boy and a girl."

He gives me a curious look. "But you'll let me read it, right? I love reading your stuff. I swear it gives me a little insight into what goes on in that head of yours."

"Which is pure madness." I do my best evil villain voice and he laughs. "And, yes, I promise you'll get to read it when it's done."

Seeming satisfied, he lies back down and gets comfortable. I only start really writing, though, when he falls asleep, otherwise I'd feel like he's watching me.

The first date was magical. They ate. They danced. They laughed. They smiled. By the end of the night, the air was so electric the girl had to glance around because it seriously felt like there were faeries hiding in the bushes, sprinkling pixie dust wherever they went.

"I'm glad we did this," the guy said as they walked up a path they'd never taken before, side by side.

"I'm glad, too," she replied. "I had a lot of fun." And it was the truth. She did have fun, and it had almost made the night surreal. Maybe she was dreaming. Maybe she'd fallen asleep and none of this was real. If that was the case then she hoped she'd never wake up.

The stars and the moon shone above them, and the houses around them were fast asleep. It was only them. No monsters. No expectations. No kingdoms and queens and kings and palaces.

It was perfect.

For the first time in a long time, the girl felt safe.

Maybe even daring.

With every ounce of bravery she could summon, she reached over and took the boy's hand in hers. She half expected him to recoil from the contact, half expected herself to do the same thing. Instead, the boy held on and she gripped tighter.

There wasn't a spark or a zap from the contact, merely a rush of energy as their flesh touched for the first time.

"You know, I never would have been here if it wasn't for you," he said so abruptly it threw her off guard.

"What do you mean?" she asked, stopping with the boy beneath a lamppost, the only light surrounding them.

He looked down at her with such passion in his eyes, begging for her to understand. "That night when you came... when you saved me, it changed the direction of my life."

The girl felt breathless. "How so?"

"Because I'd given up," he said, daring to graze his finger down her cheek, causing her to shudder and her heart to skip a beat. "I thought the world was full of monsters and there wasn't really a point in fighting them anymore. That wherever I'd go, they'd be there to break me, but you... You showed me not everyone is a monster."

"You showed me that, too," the girl replied. The boy looked at her, confused, and she wanted to explain, but she couldn't just yet.

Maybe that was the key to all this, wasn't it? Not the key to being a princess again. She didn't want to be a princess anymore, knew better than to believe in such things. But what she did want to be is a normal girl who could hold hands with a guy without feeling ugly and disgusted.

265

She only wanted to be happy in her own little world.

"I wish I could do more," he replied with a sad expression.

She didn't want him to be sad, though.

She wanted him to be happy.

The both of them.

But she had to wonder if maybe he could do more. Or maybe she had to do it herself. Maybe she was the one who had to be brave enough to save herself.

Without even thinking, she started to lean in to kiss him, hoping she wouldn't scare him. To her surprise, he leaned in too, and the two of them met in the middle.

The joining of their lips didn't set off an explosion of fireworks. There was no music announcing that this was the starting point of their happily ever after. In fact, the light above them flickered off and there was nothing except darkness. But it couldn't smother the light caused by the fire hidden deep inside each other's hearts, a fire that could quite possibly burn forever if they chose to let it.

And it was a start.

To happiness.

To a life without monsters controlling them.

And really, that's all both of them ever wanted.

Not a happily ever after.

Just a happy after.

I'm not sure how long I stare at the screen, deciding if that's it, although I'm pretty sure it's at least for an hour. After the hour is up, I decide I'm happy with it and save the story in my portfolio file. Then I lean over to put my computer aside on the floor, not wanting to get out of bed and out from beneath the covers. The room is dark, the only light coming through the window of the door where I can see the moon up in the sky.

"I forgot to give you your present," Kayden says so abruptly I let out a blood curdling scream.

"Oh, my God, you scared me." I catch my breath through his hysterical laughing. "I thought you were asleep."

"No, I've been awake." He stifles his laughter and sits up, reaching for his duffel bag beside the bed.

"This entire time?"

He unzips the bag. "Yeah, I was watching you write."

"That sounds super boring." I lie down in the bed and rotate on my side to face him.

"Actually, it was super entertaining." He grabs something from his bag, flips on a lamp nearby, and then turns to me. There's a small, silver box in his hand and a sparkle in his eyes. "Merry Christmas." He gives me the box as he lies back down beside me.

I wait a moment or two, trying not to think too hard about what's in it. Finally, I just open it.

Then I stop breathing.

"Oh, my God, you didn't have to do this..." I whisper in awe.

"I know I didn't," Kayden says, watching me with a smile on his face, "but I wanted to."

Inside the box is probably one of the coolest necklaces I've seen. It's in no way traditional, which makes me love it even more. The silver pendant is shaped like a book, and when I pick it up, I noticed that, engraved on the front, is the inscription *By Callie Lawrence*. The pendant also opens up like a locket, but the inside is blank, like fresh pages ready to be stained with a story.

"Do you like it?" Kayden finally asks, and I realize, beneath his grin, he's waiting for my approval.

"It's perfect," I reply then kiss him.

"Good," he says between kisses. "I'm glad you like it. It's for when you write your story. To show that I believe in you."

I almost start crying. "I love it." I put the necklace on, promising to never take it off. Then I lie down and snuggle against him beneath the covers, feeling more content than I ever have.

I'm about to fall asleep when he asks, "Can I read it now?"

My eyelids lift open. "Read what?"

"Your story," he says with a lopsided grin as he stares down at me expectantly. "I saw you type 'The End'."

I suddenly grow nervous, my palms so sweaty I have to wipe them off on the front of my shirt. "You want to read it right now?"

He nods enthusiastically. "I do."

"Um... okay." I turn over and reach for my laptop. I hope he likes it—hope he understands it—because, really, he's half the story.

And one of the most important parts.

He tells me I can go to sleep while he reads it, but there's no way I can shut my eyes and I end up lying there, staring at all the patches on the ceiling until he finishes. I know the exact moment he does because I can hear his breathing quicken. Then he sets the laptop aside and rolls over to me. As he just stares at me, I can't read him at all.

"So, what'd you think?" I ask, aiming for indifferent, but ending up sounding like a bundle of nerves.

He's silent for what feels like forever, each second passing almost painfully slow. "I think it's beautiful and meaningful and real," he finally says, his tone radiating every emotion he's feeling. "Although, I'm pretty sure ours gets a happily ever after."

"You think so?" I ask with a smile. "Because that's a big promise."

His smile reflects mine. "No, I know so."

And then he kisses me.

But this isn't the end of our story just yet.

In fact, it kind of feels like the beginning.

Chapter 27

#103 ~~Outrun~~ Leave Your Inner Demons behind and Find Your Love for the Game.

Kayden

It's the last game of the season and I'm feeling pretty good. Things have been amazing with Callie and I've been focusing on the future instead of the past. It's been that way for the last month, ever since I said my good-byes. I'm not happy all the time though, but then again no one ever is. I still feel the slightest bit of guilt and sadness whenever I think of my father and how it all ended, but that happens rarely.

What almost always happens is that I'm happy, not just with Callie and mine's relationship, but with myself. It took me forever to get to this place, to let go, but I've managed to find my own form of inner peace with all that happened to me. And I can honestly say that my life is great at the moment.

271

Right now, I'm fucking amped up, as I get ready to make the last play of the game. If we don't make the touchdown, we lose, but I'm not betting on us losing, In fact, I can feel it in the air, in the hollers of the crowd, in the lights that are so bright it's blinding. From the fucking way that I'm loving every minute of this.

My team is lined up and I'm waiting for the snap. My heart is thudding, my skin is damp with sweat, and my feet are ready. And my mind...

Is silent.

I hear everything around me. From the sound of the footsteps, to my coach shouting something on the sidelines. I also can hear my own voice.

You can do it.

I know you can.

My heart slams against my chest as the ball is snapped in my direction. My fingers perfectly wrap around it and then I'm running backward, looking for the perfect throw. But then I realize there's no perfect throw, but a close one. So I spring my arm back and let the ball launch from my fingers and soar away.

I let it all soar away as I breathe freely for the first time, waiting for whatever happens.　　 \

The ball climbs higher and so does my pulse. I swear the entire crowd is holding their breath, but maybe that's because I'm holding mine as I watch the ball reach its peak.

And then it drops.

And drops.

And drops.

Then it lands perfectly in the receiver's hands.

Perfect.

Touchdown!

The crowd starts cheering and so do my teammates as we win the game. And this time I join them, cheering and happy as I look up at the crowd where I know Callie is watching me with pride. But only part of my celebration is over the fact that I kicked ass. The other part is because I've finally left my inner demons behind and found my love for the game.

Epilogue

A little over a year later…

#595 Make Your Happy After Official (because it's about damn time).

Callie

Life is great. Not perfect, but life never is. Perfection would be boring anyway. Kayden and I are still living together and plan to stay that way for a very long time. Our walls are now covered in photos of us as a couple, of family, of friends. It shows how whole our lives are and how far we've both come.

There's been a lot of talk about Kayden getting drafted next year, and we did have the talk, even though it's early. It took him five minutes to lay out all the reasons why he needs me to come with him if he leaves Laramie, and it took me like a half a second to sputter that I'd follow him anywhere, that I can write anywhere since that's what I've been doing and plan to keep doing. That a life without him is a sad life I never want to have.

We have a little routine now where we alternate holi-

days between my parents' house and his brother's in Virginia. I got to meet a sober Tyler about six months ago and that was nice. And Kayden hasn't cut himself in just over a year. The sadness in his eyes is gone, except for on occasion, like when he gets a random call from his mother. He never answers them, though, or calls her back, and her voicemails are anything except persuading.

Other than the occasional sadness and silly fights, Kayden and I are going strong. He tells me every day that he loves me, and I tell him every day how important he is to me. Our happy after is working quite well for us and seems to only get better with time. It makes me excited for what the future holds—our future. Makes me excited that we have a future.

"Writing again, I see," Seth interrupts my thoughts as he strolls into my living room without knocking first. He doesn't bother to shut the door either, even though it's freezing outside and a light gust of snow is blowing in.

"What if I wouldn't have been dressed?" I joke, closing my journal. It's filled with so many pages of pen that ink is seriously starting to stain the edges.

Seth rolls his eyes. "Yeah, right. You would never be naked in your living room." He pauses then gets a scandalous look on his face. "I, on the other hand, make it a daily ritual."

Now I'm the one rolling my eyes. "Oh, whatever." I toss the journal on the coffee table as I get to my feet. "So, are you going to shut the door, or are you trying to add to my heating bill?" I grin at him.

He shakes his head, amused. "Actually, it's time to go to the game."

My forehead creases as I glance at the time on my phone. "But it's super early. Like hours early."

"I know," he says, picking up my coat from the armrest of the sofa and tossing it to me, "but I was instructed to take you there early."

"By who?" I ask as I slip my arms through the sleeves of my coat and zip it up.

"It's a secret." Then he winks at me and heads out the door, leaving me utterly confused.

I follow him outside, locking the door before I trot down the stairs behind him. There's a light frost on the ground and the air is nippy, but the sun is shining and the reflection of it against the snow makes everything sparkle. I can't help breathing in the magic-like quality before getting into the car.

Seth's grinning by the time I close the door then he starts up the engine and backs out.

"You're acting weird," I tell him as I buckle my seatbelt. "What's up?"

He shrugs as he rotates the steering wheel and turns toward the street. "Nothing."

I know Seth enough to know he's lying. "You're so full of it. What's going on…? Why are you taking me early?"

"It's a surprise," he says, pulling out onto the street.

"Please, pretty please, tell me," I beg with my hands clasped in front of me.

He shakes his head. "No way. Not this time."

"I won't tell anyone."

"It doesn't matter, Callie. I'd be mad at myself if I ruined this one for you."

I pout as I slump back in the seat. "Oh, fine. I'll play along." I fiddle with the stereo until I find a good song, then I attempt to relax, but as we pass by a bookstore, something dawns on me.

"Oh, crap." I put a hand to the base of my neck. "I forgot my necklace." It's the one Kayden gave me for Christmas that has a book pendant with my name on it.

"You'll be fine for one game, Callie," Seth brushes me off.

"No way. We have to go back. It brings him good luck whenever I wear it."

Seth chuckles as he turns off the main road and drives

toward the shiny, steel stadium. "You two and your super-stitions."

"It's not a superstition," I say, which isn't quite the truth, but Kayden swears that whenever I wear the neck-lace, it brings him good luck when he plays. Growing up with a father for a football coach, I know enough to tolerate these superstitions.

"Relax, Callie," Seth tells me as he parks near the en-trance of the stadium. "I have your necklace."

"Why do you have it?" I wonder.

There's a pause and I feel the shift in the air. Some-thing's happening. Something important.

Seth looks like he's about to cry as he reaches over, takes my hand, turns it palm up, and drops the necklace in-to it. "Don't look at it until you get into the stadium." He closes my fingers around it then sits back in his seat. "Now go."

I glance down at my hand and then at the stadium, knowing without really knowing that something magical is about to happen. Unable to form words, I get out of the car and make my journey toward the stadium with the necklace clutched in my hand. The security guard asks my name then lets me through when I tell him who I am.

I walk down the tunnel and onto the field, smiling

when I remember the night Kayden took me here over two years ago to play catch. Well, and to make out, pressed up against the field post. It seems smaller this time, less overwhelming, and I feel like I kind of belong here.

The feeling only amplifies when Kayden emerges in front of me. I take in his brown hair hanging in his gorgeous eyes that I swear can read my soul. And his lean arms and broad shoulders that hold me whenever I feel sad. Instead of his uniform, he's dressed his coat, a faded pair of jeans, and black boots, which I find a little odd since there's a game tonight.

"You made it," he says as he casually strolls across the field toward me, like this isn't at all weird.

"Yeah, but I'm wondering why I needed to make it," I say, tipping my head back to look up at him as he reaches me. "I'm guessing you and Seth have something major planned, since the two of you never plot together unless it's something epic."

"Oh, it's definitely epic," he assures me in a cocky tone, but his eyes reveal the opposite. He's nervous, and that makes me nervous.

"Okay..." My fingers tighten around the necklace that's in my hand. "Would you like to share with me what this epic thing is?"

He nods as he swallows hard, his skin suddenly paling.

"A-actually," he starts to stammer, but then clears his throat and shakes his head at himself. "Okay, let me try *that* again." We both laugh, not because this is funny but because we're nervous.

"Do you remember the last time you and I were out here?" he asks, motioning at the bleachers and then the field post.

I nod. "Yeah, I kicked your ass at catch."

He laughs, his eyes bright, but his nerves are still showing. "You did, didn't you?" He tugs his fingers through his hair. "Well, I thought I'd bring you back here to relive another good past memory since we haven't done this one before."

Is that what this is about? "You want to play catch again?"

He shakes his head. "No, I want to ask you something."

"Okay..."

I'm so confused.

And he's looking paler by the second.

"Do you have your necklace?" he asks, his voice is almost as soft as a whisper.

I nod then open my hand. "Yeah, Seth told me not to look at it until I got to the stadium." There's a pause and then he anxiously waits for me to catch on. "Oh, right." I laugh at myself as I look down at the pendant in my hand.

And then I see it.

What all of this is about.

On the front of the book pendant.

"By Callie Lawrence-Owens," I read aloud, sounding more nervous than him.

"Open it." This time, he does whisper.

With trembling fingers, I fumble with the clasp and finally get it open. The pages are no longer blank. They are filled with the promise of a story. And it's the most amazing story ever.

Your happy after.

"Yes!" I cry before he can even ask. Then I throw my arms around his neck and hug him with everything I have in me.

He laughs at me and whispers a, "thank God," sounding extremely happy as he returns my hug, giving me the best thing in the world.

Not just my happy after.

But his.

About the Author

Jessica Sorensen is a *New York Times* and *USA Today* bestselling author that lives in the snowy mountains of Wyoming. When she's not writing, she spends her time reading and hanging out with her family.

Other books by Jessica Sorensen:

The Coincidence Series:

The Coincidence of Callie and Kayden

The Redemption of Callie and Kayden

The Destiny of Violet and Luke

The Probability of Violet and Luke

The Certainty of Violet and Luke

The Resolution of Callie and Kayden

Unbeautiful (Coming Soon)

Seth & Grayson (Coming Soon)

The Secret Series:

The Prelude of Ella and Micha (Coming Soon)

The Secret of Ella and Micha

The Forever of Ella and Micha

The Temptation of Lila and Ethan

The Ever After of Ella and Micha

Lila and Ethan: Forever and Always

Ella and Micha: Infinitely and Always (Coming Soon)

The Shattered Promises Series:

Shattered Promises

Fractured Souls

Unbroken

Broken Visions

Scattered Ashes (Coming Soon)

Breaking Nova Series:

Breaking Nova

Saving Quinton

Delilah: The Making of Red

Nova and Quinton: No Regrets

Tristan: Finding Hope

Wreck Me (Coming Soon)

The Fallen Star Series (YA):

The Fallen Star

The Underworld

The Vision

The Promise

The Fallen Souls Series (spin off from The Fallen Star):

The Lost Soul

The Evanescence

The Darkness Falls Series:

Darkness Falls

Darkness Breaks

Darkness Fades

The Death Collectors Series (NA and YA):

Ember X and Ember

Cinder X and Cinder

Spark X and Cinder (Coming Soon)

The Sins Series:

Seduction & Temptation

Sins & Secrets

Lies & Betrayal (Coming Soon)

Standalones

The Forgotten Girl

Coming Soon:

Unraveling You

Entranced

Steel & Bones

Connect with me online:

jessicasorensen.com

http://www.facebook.com/pages/Jessica-Sorensen/165335743524509

https://twitter.com/#!/jessFallenStar